JOURNEY OF DECEPTION

JOURNEY OF DECEPTION

J.B. McBrayer

CHAPEL HILL

FULL-SERVICE   BOOK-MAKERS
ESTD.   1995

PRESS

This book is dedicated to all abused women.

Contents

Acknowledgments

Special thanks to Jean Gibbs, my dear friend of many years, for her unfailing support and encouragement and for keeping me on track while I wrote this book. She was also my initial proofreader and editor. I value all her insight and comments. She was kind enough to listen to my frustrations and sob stories.

This book would not have been possible without Margorie Echols. Her expertise in psychiatric nursing was immeasurable. I appreciate our discussions and her medical guidance.

The editor at Chapel Hill Press, Rena Distasio, is a special hero. She sorted through my writing and helped me make sense of my script.

Thanks to Edwina Woodbury at Chapel Hill Press for her reassurances and positive comments. This is my first time writing and publishing a book, and she was a tremendous asset and in my corner all the way.

Enjoying a hot latte, I sat waiting for Al in Java House, our favorite café in New Haven. We met there as often as time permitted. That afternoon he was late, which wasn't unusual. A professor of art history at Yale University, Al often got so involved in his work that time escaped him. As a registered nurse working in psychiatry at a mental health center in Danbury, Connecticut, about a half hour northwest of New Haven, I had a stricter relationship with time. So I waited patiently, thinking about what had recently transpired between us.

The week before, Al called and told me that he had spent a lot of time thinking about our relationship and felt that he was ready to begin a life with me. He then asked me to marry him, and I gladly accepted, right over the phone. We even started planning our wedding and honeymoon, and before we hung up Al asked me to meet him here today so he could so he could give me my engagement ring.

I fell in love with Al the first moment I met him at an art exhibit forty years ago. He seemed to me the most exciting man I'd ever met. Al was physically appealing at six feet tall, neatly groomed, energetic, and happy. A former socialite, I am fairly attractive myself, slender at five feet seven inches, blond hair with blue eyes and I've retained my curvy figure. I couldn't wait to be married to him, to have him all to myself during our honeymoon. Al suggested a tour of France, a country that I have always wanted to explore.

The art, architecture, and museums of Paris intrigue me, as does a side trip to Normandy, where an uncle of mine fought during World War II.

I spent the evening and much of that morning sharing the happy news with friends, family, and colleagues. I'm sure I bored everyone to tears with my exuberance, but they seemed happy for me. A few of my friends did voice their concerns about the difference in our ages (I am forty, and Al fifty), temperaments, and socioeconomic backgrounds. I'm a farm girl from the South, born and bred in a little town just north of the white sands of the South Carolina seashore. Al was born and bred in Brooklyn, New York, the only child of wealthy German immigrant parents. His father had been a successful gemologist and jeweler, thus giving Al a privileged upbringing that included summers at a stately second home in the Berkshires. Many people considered Al immature and restless, as if, in spite of his professional accomplishments, he were still searching for something to give his life meaning. But I found his boyishness charming, his restlessness indicative of a curious and passionate mind.

In addition to teaching courses in art history, Al was a painter and sculptor. After a fascinating conversation that ranged from art to literature and film, we realized that we had many interests in common. We embarked on a casual friendship at first, and often bumped into each other at various local events and shows. At that time, Al was divorced and I was married. Romance was far from our minds. We were simply friends with shared interests. When my marriage ended in divorce a year later because of my husband's infidelity, Al was there to offer his support. At first he was simply a shoulder to cry on over coffee. Then we started to date, at first casually, then exclusively. And now my happiness was complete. I was about to receive what I was sure would be a beautiful symbol of Al's love and devotion. Just thinking about our life together, the adventure and romance, made me as giddy as a schoolgirl.

While I waited, I chose a seat facing the door so Al could see me when he arrived. As he entered the café, his body language conveyed anxiety and his face looked troubled. I waved and smiled at him happily as he approached the table. He did not return my smile, he did not look happy, and he did not look me in the eyes. He surely did not look like a man who was about to become engaged. Something was wrong, but I couldn't fathom what it could be. We had talked last night to confirm today's meeting. He had not mentioned any problems.

"Maddie," he said curtly, his brown eyes averting my gaze. "How are you today?"

His hands, with their long fingers and tapered nails, trembled slightly as he sat down across from me. Maybe he was just overworked.

"Would you like a cup of coffee?" I offered. "I'll order you a cup."

"No thanks."

Now I knew something was wrong. Al rarely refused coffee. In fact I often joked that he was addicted.

When I asked what was wrong he blurted out without preamble, "Maddie, I'm sorry, but I can't marry you."

Before I could answer, he told me that he had been seeing a woman named Joyce and that she was pregnant.

"She says the child is mine, and I believe her. I need to do the right thing by her and our baby."

At first I could only sit there and blink at him, I was in such a shock.

"Maddie?" he said. "Say something."

When I fully realized what he was saying, I found my voice. "How dare you sleep with another woman, much less get her pregnant!" I spat out angrily. "I guess my love and the promise of our life together is not important enough to do the right thing by *me*? What about our engagement? What about our plans? I suppose that you no longer care about those either."

"I do care about you, Maddie, but I care about her, too. She is a nice person and she is carrying my child" He sighed and looked down at his hands. "I guess you could say that I got caught up in our affair."

"Give me a break," I snapped with an irate voice. "I notice that you said you cared for me, not loved me. Which partially explains why you were two-timing me, you jerk. You obviously didn't care enough about me not to see another woman. Does this Joyce person know that you were cheating on her with me?"

"No, she doesn't know about you, nor does she suspect," he said, keeping his gaze on the table and running his hands through his curly dark hair, which had remained full and thick.

"Well, that's just great. I guess I should be happy that you have no loyalty to either of us, you deceptive scoundrel!" I said, my voice reaching near-hysterical levels.

Al never could handle it when I got angry, so he quickly rose from the table and came around to my side. As I stood, he reached out as if to hug me. Then I slapped him on his face as hard as I could and threw my coffee at him. "Never, ever touch me again."

"Damn it, Madeline, these are my best pants. That's going to stain. What is wrong with you?"

"What is wrong with *me*? Do you really not have any idea, or are you just being obtuse?"

"Don't get angry," Al said. "I still want to be friends. We can see each other from time to time. My marriage should not prevent that."

I couldn't believe what I was hearing. The night before, the man had asked me to marry him. Now he was telling me that couldn't happen because another woman was pregnant with his baby. But he still wanted to be friends? It was all too much. I needed to get out of there.

"I don't know what kind of woman you think I am, but I'm not interested in an affair. Does Joyce know about this side of you? Maybe I should call her and tell her."

"Look," he said. "We don't have to have an affair. Just meet and talk or see a play now and then. Come on, Maddie. I care a lot about you and would like to continue seeing you. I enjoy being with you. We don't need to change anything. I just can't marry you right now. And there's no reason to call Joyce. I doubt she would believe you and would just think you were jealous."

Astonished, I ranted, "Al, you are full of crap. Do you know how stupid you sound? How did you ever earn a doctorate?"

The other customers were staring now. I had to leave quickly. Trying to show pride rather than devastation, I held my head high as I rushed from the café. Once outside, I finally let the tears fall. I felt like I would die from profound heartbreak. I was hurt to the core, emotionally and psychologically empty. The day that had begun with such promise and excitement had ended in a way I had never expected.

I have no memory of how I got home, but once inside I started to shake uncontrollably. I was freezing cold. His words had me reeling with shock. If my problems had been from physical causes I feel sure I would have ended up in the emergency room of a local hospital. I rushed into the bathroom to draw a hot bath, and forced myself to look in the mirror. My blue eyes were swollen and rimmed bright red from crying. My skin had paled to the color of ash. Despite being cold, beads of sweat dotted my forehead and upper lip. My long blond hair, which I'd so carefully styled that morning in anticipation of my meeting with Al, now hung limp around my shoulders, its curls deflated as my dreams.

The hot bath stopped my shaking and chills, but I couldn't relax. Maybe sleep would be my savior. But once in bed, my mind kept spinning as I tried desperately to figure out what went wrong. I asked myself what I had done to cause our broken engagement. I asked myself what this Joyce had that made her so special. I tossed and turned, sleep as elusive as the answers to my questions.

By morning I still felt numb. My mind knew that it was over between us, but my heart refused to accept that Al would no longer be in my life. I had no idea how I would cope, and now I didn't even have the assistance of anger. At some point during the night, my anger had disappeared, leaving only the pain of rejection and loss. That would take a long time to resolve.

I hadn't cursed Al to hell in the café, but now that I was alone I called him every despicable name in the book, pacing the floor and not caring if the neighbors heard. He had earned every word I spewed forth. I put the blame totally on Al. This was his fault—I had done nothing wrong but love him.

Now I was angry with myself. How could I have been so blind? I was angry at Al for betraying me and at myself for letting myself be duped by him. He had hidden his other life well, but why had I never suspected anything? I knew he was charming. I knew he had a way with women, but it had never occurred to me that he would betray our trust. Had we married he would have continued to see Joyce, and perhaps other women, too, and I would have been clueless. What if she had gotten pregnant then? The what-ifs were mind-boggling. Our marriage would have been a lie.

I knew I had to go forward and continue my life without Al in it. I had survived duplicity before—the dissolution of my ten-year marriage to my college sweetheart—and I would survive Al's duplicity now, but that was not what I wanted nor was it how I responded to hurt. In reality, I really wanted to lash out, cause pain, and hurt him, too. But I didn't know how and I didn't think he cared enough to *be* hurt. At some point in his life I believed he would get his comeuppance. What goes around comes around. Maybe the steamroller of karma was parked in his driveway waiting for the right moment to roll over him.

What I did know for certain was that my life had changed in the blink of an eye. Explaining my changed circumstances to people would be difficult and embarrassing. While I did not want my friends and family to feel sorry for me, I knew they would. It's human nature. Everyone knew how much I loved Al, but I also knew they would be there for me if needed.

Basically, I knew I would be alright. One day my life would feel worthwhile and have order again. Many people have been through what I went through. I just never imagined it would happen to me.

Chapter One

Twenty years later

OVER THE NEXT TWENTY YEARS, I caught occasional glimpses of Al around New Haven and even Danbury. I had heard through the grapevine that he'd married Joyce months after we broke up, but he was always by himself when I saw him, and it was always at a distance.

I often wondered how I would react if I did see him face-to-face. One spring afternoon I found out. We literally ran into each other. I was leaving Yale's library as he was going in. I recognized him instantly but didn't want him to recognize me. "Please excuse me," I said, keeping my head down and moving past him quickly.

Not quickly enough.

Al did a double take and then exclaimed, "Madeline!"

I kept moving, but he turned around and caught up with me. "This is a nice surprise. I didn't know you lived in New Haven, or are you just visiting? Do you still live in Danbury?"

I kept walking. "I'm well, thanks. But I'm busy and need to get going."

Al reached out as if to grab my arm and then seemed to think better of it. "Hang on for just a minute. Let's have coffee sometime and talk, okay?"

My heart pounding, I stopped and spit back at him, "What, do you want to ruin another pair of pants?" Then I turned and continued walking at a brisk pace toward the parking lot. Al didn't follow me.

Once inside my car, my hands shook as I tried to turn on the ignition. I took a couple deep breaths to calm myself. I always knew there was a chance we'd run into each other, and I was surprised that it had taken twenty years, given how much I enjoyed visiting Yale's art gallery and library.

Obviously, Al still had the same effect on me, even though he was older. Twenty years makes a difference. Age, marriage, and fatherhood, of course, had taken their toll, but regardless of the lines etched into his face he was still handsome at nearly seventy years old, still had the same bounce in his step and great posture. The gray-streaked hairs in his stylish haircut looked distinguished, not dowdy. His beard was neatly trimmed. Aging is a peculiar experience, and most of us do not think that it applies to us individually. I wonder what he thought when he saw me? Did he think I had aged, too? Sixty hardly qualifies as old these days, and I had tried to take care of myself, but I was not that young, starry-eyed girl he'd first met all those years ago. At that moment, I realized that I still cared for him, still cared what he thought of me. "No!" I said out loud, clutching the steering wheel. I would *not* go down that path.

Months later, a mutual acquaintance gave Al my phone number. Because I didn't know his number, I picked up the first time he called—and then promptly hung up on him when he identified himself. After that, I let his calls go straight to voicemail.

But the man was nothing if not persistent. One day I decided to pick up the phone and put a stop to this nonsense.

"What?" I barked at him.

Al laughed. "Easy. I just called to see how you were doing. I had hoped we'd run into each other again at Yale."

Actually, he wanted me to know how *he* was doing. I sensed that he was lonely, and as much as I hated to admit it, so was I. During our conversation, he told me that he and Joyce had "called it quits" fifteen years into their marriage. They had decided to share custody of their child, a girl who favored her mother. Being a father was harder than he had imagined. From there, we went on to talk about his daughter and stepdaughter from Joyce's previous marriage and what had happened in his life in the past twenty years. He made it a point to tell me he'd been single since the divorce. He never asked me about my life. Regardless, our conversation did have meat. We didn't just talk about mundane things, and I realized then just how much I missed stimulating conversation. I hadn't dated anyone seriously in the past twenty years. Mostly I socialized with colleagues at the hospital in Danbury. But I needed more than just shop talk.

After that phone call, I agreed to meet him for coffee. Something always seemed unfinished between us since we never discussed his marriage. Eventually we did talk about our breakup. Though he never really apologized, he did say, "I know I treated you badly, Maddie. I was trapped in my deception and didn't know a good way out."

"You put me through a horrible time, more horrible than you will ever know," I said quietly. "Why should I believe you now? I imagine you are still looking for women. One was not enough for you all those years ago. Do you still need at least two?"

He denied that he was playing the field. As our conversation progressed, he opened up more and more to me, trying to explain his behavior, and I opened up more and more to him, trying to get him to understand just how deeply he'd hurt me. Our past was finally out in the open, and I wanted to keep our association that way as well. Perhaps he truly did understand what he had done to me.

Chapter Two

ALTHOUGH MY PROFESSIONAL LIFE had been immensely satisfying these past twenty years, something had been missing in my personal one. There had been a few men over the years, but no one serious or long-term. So maybe that was why I gave in and met Al for dinner: I was lonely and craving the company of the opposite sex. We were starting over, slowly learning about each other as we went along, which is how I wanted it to be. I was guarding myself. Self-preservation was of utmost importance, now more than ever. Still, many years had passed since Al and I had been close. Both of us were different people now, changed in more than just looks. Surely he was a different man?

After nearly thirty years as a professor of art history, Al was now thinking of retiring. He was tired of the academic rat race, as he called it. I on the other hand enjoyed my professional life and planned to continue working as a nurse for at least another ten years. Helping others was tremendously rewarding. Besides, I was not ready for such a large step. I knew I would get bored easily without something to give my life daily purpose.

As the months progressed, I slowly began to let my guard down. Al and I became close again. We went out to dinner, took the train to New York to see Broadway plays, went to the movies, and attended various seminars. Having someone to pal around with was nice. Al was attentive and fun to be with. He seemed unchanged in many ways, and I really enjoyed our excursions and discussions.

One day out of the blue, Al said, "You know, since my divorce I have been trying to find someone I can connect with. Now you have come back into my life, and I realize that I relate to you better than anyone I know. I've enjoyed spending time with you. I hurt you once, and I don't want to do that again."

With these words, my resolve crumbled. For reasons I could not explain, and despite our history and my anger and pain, I knew that I still cared about this man. Maybe I was even falling in love with him again. When he told me there were no longer women in his life, I smiled, wanting to believe him. My heart warmed to him, and even though he had never asked for my forgiveness, I was willing to give it—even if I could not forget. But maybe I could find a way to live with those memories of hurt and pain while moving toward a better future.

One day in August Al came to visit me in Danbury. We sat at my kitchen table, drinking tea and chatting about a movie we'd seen recently. Suddenly, Al turned serious. "Maddie, I'm still thinking of retiring and am making plans about what to do afterward. One option I'm considering is to live at my house in the Berkshires full-time."

He paused, as if expecting me to say something. When I didn't, he continued, the words spilling out in a rush. "Would you consider coming to live with me? I've missed you, and am now realizing just how much. The house seems lonesome and quiet with just me in it. I know you remember the house. Let's travel, enjoy our retirement, and grow old together."

Stunned at this announcement, I released the breath I had been holding and said, "Al, I don't know what to say. We've only just started to get reacquainted, and now you want me to move in with you?"

"I know you must be surprised," he said. "Living together would be a major change for both of us. We are more set in our ways now than we were years ago, but we're also not strangers to each other. I don't know about you, but I don't look forward to spending the future alone."

"Being alone is not always fun," I responded, "but being miserable together would be worse. It's not so bad, living by oneself—as I have discovered."

"Maddie, our living together will not be miserable. We can make it special. We will be able to take nice vacations together and enjoy our lives. My house is plenty large enough for both of us."

"Al, I once cared deeply for you, but so much has happened since then. Our lives have changed, and we are different people in many ways. Living together requires serious consideration, and I would have to give up a lot to live with you—much more than you would have to give up. To be perfectly honest, I still have distrust issues to resolve within myself. You need to prove to me that you are trustworthy."

Al put his right hand over his heart. "You can trust me, Maddie. My old ways are over. My house is big, too big for one person. We can ramble around in it together while making it our home. Maybe we can restore it. Someday I would like to establish an art gallery in the lower level. I have wanted to do that for years. You can help with that. I value your input."

"Al, I don't know what to say."

He reached across the table to take my hands. "Maddie, I hope you'll seriously consider my offer. You have always had a warm place in my heart. I still care deeply for you."

"Living together is not a venture to take lightly," I said. "And I still don't trust you."

Al replied, "From now on I want you to feel safe and secure with me. I tell you, I am a changed man. I have often wondered what would have happened to us if we had married. I want to believe that our lives would have been better."

"I have often wondered the same thing," I said, shaking my head, "but we will never know now. The door to the possibility of marriage closed long ago for me."

For weeks I gave the matter serious thought, and Al and I had a number of long follow-up conversations. Deep down I felt that it would be primarily my responsibility to make our relationship work. When we broke up years before, I knew that I had not caused the problems between us. He is the one who had cheated, although a small part of me often wondered if there had been anything I could have done to keep him by my side, if something was lacking in me. This time I would try to please him in every way I knew how. We had never lived together—maybe that would make a difference. Admittedly, I was by now back in love with him. But did he love me? He hadn't used that word yet. He never had. Was it because he couldn't say it or because he couldn't *feel* it? Whatever the case, my shattered heart had healed, and I did not want him to break it again.

I called Julie, one of the women with whom I'd gone to nursing school and now my closest friend, to discuss my situation. Julie and I also had geography in common. Although I was born and raised in Little River, South Carolina, I knew Julie's hometown of Wilmington, North Carolina, well. The charming old port city had been a popular destination for my girl-friends and me during high school. While I hadn't known Julie back then, finding out she was not only from the South but also from Wilmington helped cement our bond even further while in school. Upon graduation, we reluctantly went our separate ways. I accepted a job in Danbury, and Julie remained in Wilmington. Although Julie had never married, a string of long-term relationships had made her wise in the ways of the heart.

"Maddie," Julie said, "are you out of your mind? I don't understand how you could even think about living with him."

"I know it's crazy to even contemplate this drastic of a change, but I have searched my heart and I know that I still love him. I'm not ignoring the past, but he says he is a changed man, and I believe him. We are older now and we have both changed. I think living together will help bring our relationship closer."

Julie sighed loudly. "You see something in him that I don't and never have. Living together is not always a good thing and is not always as romantic as it's touted to be. And I don't know if you truly believe him or just *want* to believe him. I can tell by your voice that you are excited about him. Whatever you decide, you have my support. I just don't want to see you hurt again. If he does hurt you I'll jerk a knot in his head and tie a bow in it."

"I will definitely keep that in mind," I said, laughing at the colorful southern expression. Then I thanked her for being there for me and promised I'd let her know as soon as I made a decision.

I did not take the matter of living with Al lightly; it took me months to decide. As I had requested, Al did not push me to make a decision. After much soul-searching, I finally had to be honest and admit that I wanted someone in my life again, someone special. I felt sure that this time, Al would be that person. His past betrayal was just that: in the past. I could not forget, but I could forgive. As I told Julie, I had looked deeply into my heart before agreeing to live with him. Al and I were comfortable with each other and seemed to be compatible.

Eventually, after weeks of talks, Al and I came to an understanding about what our relationship would be and how we would organize our lives together. With a positive attitude and happy outlook for the future, I drew up a contract dictating how we would live together. We agreed that I would have my own studio and a private bath, and our finances and wills were to remain separate. We were both to share the responsibility of cooking and cleaning; I would not be picking up after him. We were to be partners, with the possibility of marriage in the future. Either way, our cohabitation would be as a married couple. We would care for one another during illness; we would respect one another, address any conflicts, and most importantly, we would never commit adultery. We both agreed and signed it. A signed contract was important to me.

Once we put pen to paper, Al kissed me and said, "I've missed you, Maddie, and I'm glad I found you again. There are so many things I want us to share. You will bring life to the house. In fact, think of it as yours as well as mine. Decorate it as you see fit. It can use some sprucing up and a woman's touch. You'll know just what to do."

His words were like music to my ears, but for some reason I dragged my feet. I'd agreed to his proposal, he'd agreed to the terms of the contract, but when it came to moving out of my house and into his, I took my time. I knew I would be giving up a great deal of my independence, in spite of Al assuring me I would have my own set of rooms and an entire bathroom to myself.

So I stalled by telling Al I wanted to take some time to get my house ready to put on the market. I spent the next month having the inside repainted, the floors polished, the windows washed, and the carpets steamed. I felt a pang of sadness when the Realtor finally planted the for-sale sign on my front lawn. I'd lived contentedly in that house for twenty-five years, and even though I'd lived there alone, it had been my place and no one else's. When it sold only two weeks after being on the market, that sealed the deal. No more stalling. Putting aside all doubts, I hired a local company to load a U-Haul and hitch it to my car. Then I hit the road to Al's family home, Twin Oaks, in Oak Ridge, New York, in the Berkshires.

Chapter Three

IN THE EARLY FALL, when I arrived at Twin Oaks—so named because of the towering oak trees on each side of the house—, I was shocked to see just how rundown it looked from the outside. The gardens were overgrown, paint was chipping off the house, and the porch was sagging. It reminded me of an abandoned house in my neighborhood growing up, one that we kids considered haunted and always refused to walk past. Puzzled by the neglect, I wasn't even sure that I was at the correct address. How could Al have let his ancestral estate lay in such ruin? Had his parents been living, they surely would have been shocked and disappointed.

I knew that I should have gone to visit before agreeing to move in. "Needs a little sprucing up," as Al had put it, is entirely different from "needs a complete renovation," as I was now seeing it. This was not a positive way to begin our life together.

Al met me on the front porch with a big smile on his face, put his arm around my waist, and ushered me inside. The boards creaked beneath my feet, and I wondered if they would hold me up. The outside was not the worst of it. When I entered the large foyer I surveyed my surroundings with astonishment. There were water stains on the plaster walls, the wooden floors needed refinishing, and the carpet on the stairs leading upstairs was faded and threadbare. And that was just what I saw in my immediate surroundings. I didn't want to think about what I would see in the living areas, the kitchen, and the upstairs bedrooms.

Pulling away from Al's embrace, I blurted out, "Al, this place is a mess! 'Sprucing up' doesn't even begin to describe what this house needs." It took everything I had not to walk right back out the door. "I can't believe that you invited me to live in a pigsty."

"You have had a major leak. Where did all the water come from? Did a pipe break? It looks like it happened a while ago." He replied, "A pipe broke in the upstairs bathroom some time ago.

At least he had the decency to look embarrassed. "There just seems more to do than I can handle. It's pretty overwhelming."

"Then why in the world didn't you hire a caretaker?"

Al just shrugged.

"Or is that what I am? Am I the only woman, out of all those that you know, who has a 'woman's touch'—or am I just the only one stupid enough to have agreed to come here?"

Al shook his head. "Yes, okay, I admit that I wanted you to help me fix this place up. Because I think you'd be really good at it and would enjoy making it your own as well as mine. I never thought about a caretaker and wouldn't have known where to find one anyway. See, you already have a good idea. The insurance company reimbursed me for the water damage, but I haven't taken the time to have everything repaired. You'll know what to do—you're great at this sort of thing. But let me be clear, I wanted you here primarily because I missed you."

"Al, walking into a mess like this is not a good way for me to begin my life with you. Have you thought about that? What have you been doing with your time? Homes need love and attention. This is a beautiful and historical property, and you've neglected it."

"I've been working at the university and living in New Haven," he said, a defensive tone sneaking into his voice. "You know how that goes."

I wanted to ask how Joyce could have raised their child in such a place, but decided it was best to stay away from that topic, knowing it was a sore subject. I knew that he rarely saw his girls. They had their own lives and had sided with their mother in the divorce. His stepdaughter, Amy, was at Columbia working toward her law degree, and his daughter, Megan, was studying music at Julliard. Instead of bringing them up, I continued my rant. "Did you think that your parents' long-dead servants would magically return and clean up your mess once more? You could have at least hired someone to paint the outside and caulk and fix the windows. They look like they're ready to fall out. Finding someone to clean up the yard would not have taken a lot of investigating."

Al came from a wealthy family and had inherited money along with the manor house. His family's friends were upper crust from New York City. German was spoken in the home, and traditional German foods were served. Having grown up with caretakers and servants, Al had never learned to be handy around the house. His privileged upbringing had made him naïve to the hard work that was necessary to keep a house like this in good condition.

"I know, Maddie. All this damage occurred after Joyce and the children moved out. But the house needed refreshing while she was here. We were both busy with our careers. I'm just not good at this sort of thing, and I haven't taken the time. Upstairs isn't too bad. Most of the water damage is down here. Everything doesn't have to be done at once. We can do it gradually. Together. Having you here will boost my energy and enthusiasm."

I sighed. "Okay, Al. We'll take this one day at a time. But I need your commitment to help, and I need you to be aware of what the costs will be. It won't be inexpensive."

"I know that," he said, "and of course we'll use my money on all the repairs. I'll put your name on my credit card and arrange it so you can write checks on my account. That should cover everything."

"Good," I said. I didn't plan to spend a cent of my money. "Setting things right will take a lot of time. I need to think about the best way to go about this, where to start first. Right now, though, thinking about it just makes me tired."

"Maddie, I know you can accomplish a lot with my home. Think of it as a challenge, not a problem."

I rolled my eyes. *Yeah, right*, I thought. Hopefully, this was the only thing Al had neglected to share with me. The only thing that gave me comfort was that Twin Oaks was now my home as well. Since I planned to live here, and refused to live in a mess, I needed to immediately begin the process of arranging repairs. I would probably not accomplish much before returning to my part-time nursing job in Danbury the next week.

Although I was exhausted, I spent the next hour walking from room to room to further assess the damage. I would make in-depth notes at another time. For now I just wanted to get a general handle on what I was dealing with. No doubt, as a Federal-style home built in the 1890s and located just outside the village of Oak Ridge, Twin Oaks was solidly constructed and beautifully designed. With four chimneys and banks of tall windows on each floor, the house was evidence of a time long passed, when the fireplaces were the sole sources of heat and summertime breezes cooled the interiors. At one time, it must have been a showstopper. That was the good news. The bad news was that it would take time, effort, and lots of money to restore it. I hardly knew where to begin.

Talking more to myself than to Al, I said, "It seems like the first step would be to hire a contractor to assess the damage and give us a rundown of the cleaning and repair costs. Then once everything is clean and in basic working order, find a designer to help restore it to its original condition." I was getting excited now. Maybe this *would* be possible, given enough careful planning. "And that art gallery you mentioned to me," I continued, addressing Al directly. "We could incorporate that into the renovation as well."

"Take your time," Al said, following me like an eager puppy. "Do what you think best. I'm just happy you're here. Everything will work out."

My thoughts were on the repairs while Al and I unloaded my car and the trailer. Then I familiarized myself with the house and where Al kept things, kitchen first. Luckily I had taken two weeks off from work to make the move, and I would take that time to get organized, assess the damage, and decide what to tackle first. I tried not to think too far ahead, tried not to feel overwhelmed.

The house was two main stories. The ground floor contained a large foyer and living room, music room, and bathroom. Three additional rooms included the main kitchen, a butler's pantry, and a formal dining room with a huge crystal chandelier and a beautifully carved oak table with seating for twelve. A small reading room was just off the kitchen. Al's parents had used these rooms often, entertaining a bevy of friends and colleagues, who included everyone from musicians and composers to doctors and politicians. Al and I would also use the rooms for entertaining, but on a much lesser scale.

A curved stairway led to the upper level. This less formal section of the house was where Al and I would live, as had his parents. The area contained an adequate kitchen with an eating area, a large family room that opened onto a spacious deck, three full baths, a half bath, and four bedrooms. The house included a finished basement and attic that had not been used in years, except for storage. The estate sat on twelve treed acres, with the house occupying a prime spot on a gently sloping hill that was surrounded by gardens and large swaths of lawn both front and back.

I was surprised at how much I'd been able to get done within just a few days. I cleaned up the bedroom that Al and I shared, an airy master suite at the end of the hall on the second floor, and then went to work on the adjoining bathroom, which Al had assured me I could have all to myself. He would take the one down the hall, between the second and third bedrooms. I also gave the kitchen a thorough scrubbing and removed the cabinet doors to clean the cabinets out. Al wanted me to leave them off, he said it was too much trouble to open a cabinet door. I ignored him. I also bought a bright yellow tablecloth for the small table that stood by a bank of bay windows and gave the wooden chairs a good polish. At least part of the house was livable until I could start calling contractors.

In spite of Al telling me to wait, the more I thought about it, the more sense it made to incorporate the art gallery into the restoration. The downstairs living room, a large space with floor-to-ceiling windows, would be perfect. And because that room was in relatively good condition compared to the rest of the house, it would be the last and most fun of the projects—a good way to end what I knew would be an exhausting undertaking. The gallery would display our paintings and Al's sculptures. Various upholstered benches would be placed around the room, and I could already picture the pedestal tables that would brighten up the room by holding fresh flowers.

I also took on the process of getting the house listed on the National Register of Historic Places, a new adventure for me. Due to the age of the house, I knew it qualified for historic recognition. I began researching the process, looking into requirements and how to become nominated. I had never lived in an old, historic home before now, and it was exciting.

Finally, I began to explore the grounds of the estate. A short walk from the back of the house led to the top of another hill at the edge of the property, offering picturesque views of the valley below and the stream that ran through it. When the wind was right I could hear the rushing water. Since the acreage had never been fenced, wildlife, including numerous deer, roamed freely.

The whole area was just beautiful. Growing up, Al had called this old house home, even though he and his family also had a modest apartment in Brooklyn, New York. He told me of winters spent at Twin Oaks, of sunshine glistening on the boughs of the towering pines, and of sledding parties with neighborhood children. I fell in love with those stories and was looking forward to the day when we would add our own memories to the history of the house.

Chapter Four

Every day it seemed that I rushed from one room to another trying to accomplish my goals before heading to Danbury. Some days I took a break from the inside labors to work in the gardens. Weeds were prolific, and I attacked them as if they were my enemies. But I enjoyed being out of doors, and unlike the scrubbing I'd been doing inside, preparing flower beds was both fun and relaxing. The weather would be cold soon, and I wanted at least part of the garden chores completed.

Visitors would have thought I was a bum, given my choice of clothing: faded denim with holes in the knees and oversized men's shirts that had seen better days. But none of the neighbors came to welcome me, which was fine. Not only did I look a mess, I couldn't spare the time to chitchat. I had too much to do before returning to work.

Regardless of my fatigue, I felt a sense of satisfaction as the house, yard, and gardens took shape. One day everything would be beautiful again. Seeing the finished product would be a dream come true. Although I was often discouraged and almost always aggravated, I was not unhappy.

Al was on fall break from the university, so we were able to talk daily about the work. He seemed not to mind the outside work as long as I was with him. While I weeded and planted, he cut the low branches from the trees and pulled brush from the gardens. The work gave him the opportunity to use his prized tractor, which for some reason he'd named Gertrude, or Old Gertie when he was feeling especially fond of the machine. He would hitch the trailer to the tractor, load it up with debris, and away he would go, hauling everything into the woods. He liked to rev the tractor into high gear and speed down the lane, grinning at me like a kid on a racetrack. On occasion he'd offer me a ride. I'd stand behind him, holding on tight, but he never played the speed demon when I was with him. Whether working or playing, he was fun.

That's because working outside made him happy. In addition to operating Old Gertie, he also cut down and sawed up a rotting tree with his chainsaw. I was afraid of the thing and would never have tried to operate it, but Al wielded the noisy, rattling saw with dexterity and confidence. Good thing, too, because now we'd have plenty of wood for the winter. I imagined how toasty and cozy our rooms would feel with fires glowing in each of the old stone fireplaces. And I knew Al couldn't wait to start plowing snow with Old Gertie. Winter was coming sooner than we wanted, we were so preoccupied working to get the house and gardens in order.

After our work was finished we would pull up a couple chairs on the porch, sit back with cups of tea, and enjoy the feeling of accomplishment that came from jobs well done.

Unfortunately, Al tired of our work after only several days. By that Friday he begged off, saying he had to get up to New Haven to prepare for a class for the upcoming semester, which started in a couple of weeks. Sure, it had all been fun and games when he was riding his tractor and using his chainsaw, but now that we were getting down to the nitty-gritty of cleaning the other rooms in preparation for interviewing contractors, he was losing steam.

"Maddie, you are a hard taskmaster," he said. "You see it all as progress, but I see it as drudgery."

"Well, Al, you could have taken care of this mess long ago, so don't complain to me. There's a long list of work that needs to be done before we can even hire someone to do the restoration, drudgery or not."

I knew he wanted to escape. He needed his "space," as he was fond of saying, and honestly, he was getting on my nerves. "Good grief, you're like a child. I didn't ask for this job. I was roped into it. So, yeah, go on back to New Haven. Just get out of my way."

So off he went to New Haven, leaving me to work on the renovation and to make sure all the bills associated with Twin Oaks were paid on time and out of his account. Al also had a springer spaniel, Muffin, and a calico cat, George, that needed taking care of as well. I didn't mind that he was gone. I could accomplish more with him out of the way. Maybe his mood would improve with the change of scenery. He might have been concerned about his upcoming class—he was a stickler for preparation. I gave him the benefit of the doubt, but wished he took as much pride in his home as he did in his classes.

It took awhile to sort through the mess of bills, and it took precious time away from working on the house. I did not know that side of Al. Maybe, I thought, most men were that disorganized. My experience was limited. I had only lived with my father, my two brothers, and my former husband. So I accepted this side of Al and didn't say anything. We were both still in the honeymoon phase of our relationship. Soon enough I would learn that Al had a habit of leaving when things got difficult. He was terrible at dealing with things head-on. Being with his students and colleagues gave him a sense of purpose and a positive outlook. Working in the university's lab with all the equipment allowed him to sculpt, paint, and take advantage of the library.

Eventually we found a compatible course. I hired a contractor I felt I could trust, and he presented us with a renovation schedule and an estimate that met with our expectations and Al's budget. I put the house in the contractor's hands and went back to work, making the hour-and-a-half trek to Danbury on Mondays, where I would stay in an extended-stay motel suite through Friday. I also owned a ladies' dress and accessories boutique that was run by two friends. I rarely worked there, but did go by when I was in the area to check in on things. Weekends I worked to restore the home's gardens. I'd been raised on my family's farm and felt confident in my abilities to bring the manor's natural environment back to life.

Al, however, did not fully retire. Making that final decision was difficult. Like me, he found his work rewarding. But he was down to teaching only one class, so at least he was home on the weekends.

After several years together I knew my decision to live with Al had been the right one. Al was the same Al whom I had known and loved for so long. We seemed to be happy and content. I had regained my trust in him and was glad he was back in my life.

As promised, Al made time to take me on a few adventures. He had a reliable sitter for Muffin and George, so we were free to travel without worrying about them. France was still a place I wanted to visit, but it would have to wait. Instead, we took short trips close to home. One was to Niagara Falls on the American side. The falls are always spectacular. On our way home we visited Fort Niagara in Youngstown, New York. At nearly three hundred years old, Fort Niagara is the oldest continuously occupied military site in North America and is now a state park. Originally built by the French in 1726, it fell into British hands during the French and Indian War thirty years later, and then was ceded to the United States after the American War for Independence. Strolling the grounds and browsing in the gift shops was a pleasurable way to spend a short vacation. Next we took a trip to the National Baseball Hall of Fame and Museum in Cooperstown, New York. Neither of us were sports enthusiasts, but Al had grown up within a short subway ride to both Yankee Stadium and Ebbets Field, before the Dodgers relocated to Los Angeles, and had attended several games in his youth. The Dodgers were still in New York when Al was growing up. Now they call Los Angeles home. Afterward we ambled over to Hyde Hall, built by famed eighteenth-century architect Philip Hooker for wealthy landowner George Clarke. Patterned after Mr. Clarke's childhood home in England, it was the largest private residence in existence in the United States at the time it was built. As I walked through the rooms, studying the furnishings and accessories, I couldn't help but think of Twin Oaks.

Later on we ventured outside the United States, on trips to the Caribbean and to Montreal. Belize was also in our plans. Big or small, all our adventures were exciting and romantic. Every place we went was beautiful. I snapped one photo after another. Some I would use for painting themes. Painting had always been a hobby of mine, and thanks to my photographs, I now had many ideas to expand on.

The Caribbean cruise was the most relaxing of all our vacations. We had been very busy, and the winter getaway was just what we needed— seven whole days of luxury.

There's nothing like a vacation to spark renewed interest in one's partner. We spent an afternoon in our cabin, trying out the twin beds, ordering in, and laughing together like young lovers. Once we ventured outside our room, we found the ship was full of exciting and interesting activities, top-notch entertainment, and so much delicious food and drink, there was no way to sample even a fraction of what was on offer.

But the most amusing thing was watching Al gaze at the parade of oiled bikini bodies that passed by us as we lounged poolside. Al's sunglasses could not hide his interest, and I laughed at him as he tried, and failed, to look discreet. They paid him no attention.

"They're too young for you, Al," I mocked. "They must think we're their parents' ages, if they even notice us at all."

"Come on, Madeline," Al said. "We don't look old. I feel as frisky as I did fifteen years ago. I thought some poor lonely thing might need sunscreen on her back."

I laughed, and mentally cut him some slack. After all, who wouldn't feel frisky given those refreshing ocean breezes and all that sun? And Al had been getting frisky with *me* just fine; I wasn't going to be upset if he cast the occasional admiring glance at some young thing as she went walking by.

Once we were back home, we both found it difficult to return to our normal daily routines. We had been spoiled—travel obviously agreed with us. The sun had been wonderful, and we felt rejuvenated. So we planned another series of trips for the following year, including one back home to South Carolina in late spring. Although my parents were no longer living, and the family farm on which I and my sister and two brothers had grown up had been sold to developers years ago, I still had friends and family in and around the town of Little River whom I tried to visit every couple years.

Our vacation in South Carolina would be our first visit together to my home state. Al and I had been together five years by that time, and my family had yet to meet him. In the past, he'd preferred to stay home when I went to visit, which had been fine with me. But now it was time to make a showing as a couple.

I was proud of Al and wanted to show him off to my family and friends. Even though they knew about our broken engagement years before, they were not the type to hold grudges. I was happy now, that was all that mattered to them. They were looking forward to meeting him, and Al seemed happy to be making the trip as well. Or so I thought. To my surprise and dismay, the Al that emerged during this sojourn would turn out to be entirely different from the man with whom I had lived peacefully and happily for the past five years. Instead, the Al that emerged bore a striking resemblance to the Al who had broken my heart in our youth. Only now he was twenty-five years older and should have long outgrown that kind of behavior.

Chapter Five

THE SOUTH'S MAY WEATHER would be warmer and the humidity lower, too. July and August would tell a different weather version. Spring was an ideal time to travel. Warmer weather would be wonderful. It should help us thaw out again from our long, cold northern winter. South Carolina was not the Caribbean; it was better. It was home.

The day before we set out, we spent the night at Al's home in New Haven in order to be closer to the train station. We set out at the crack of dawn and were about ten minutes away from the station when I was startled out of my reverie by the shrieking of Al's cell phone. *Who in the world could be calling him this early in the morning?* He seldom used the thing, and I had forgotten that he even had it. My first thought was that there had to have been some kind of emergency.

Al answered the call. "Good morning," he said calmly. I heard a voice at the other end but couldn't tell if it was male or female. "Good, good, but I'm busy right now. Can I call you back when I have more time?"

The voice at the other end grew louder, more urgent, but I still couldn't make out if it was a man or a woman. "I'm sorry to hear it. Look, I've been busy preparing for a class, but I'll call you next chance I get."

The voice continued, lower now. "Okay, that sounds good. Talk to you soon." Al hung up.

"Al, you're not preparing for a class," I said, trying to keep my voice neutral. "And who on earth would be calling at this hour of the day?"

Al scratched his beard distractedly. "Oh, that was my old friend Carol."

It felt like my heart had dropped to my stomach—the same heart I had given him years ago and that he had left in shambles. Immediately, there was a slight crack in it again.

"Is this the same Carol you dated years ago? Who works part-time in the admissions office at Yale?"

"Yes, the same one," he replied.

I let a few seconds go by. "Why on earth is she calling you, and why so early?"

Al sighed, "I don't know. She's going through a hard time."

"How do you know that?"

"Because we talk almost every day that I am at the university. Sometimes we meet for lunch."

Now my heart was doing backflips in my stomach. "You mean to tell me that you talk to her every day and that you even meet for lunch and have been doing that for *years*? You don't even call *me* every day."

"Maddie, can we talk about this later?" Al asked as he pulled into the train station parking lot.

"Al, you said you'd never be unfaithful to me again."

"I haven't been unfaithful you," Al said evenly, turning off the engine. "Talking and going out to lunch is not being unfaithful."

"Oh yes it is, especially if you choose not to tell me. Does she know that I am in your life, that we *live* together?"

Al shrugged. "I have never made a big deal about our life together." Then he got out of the car, opened the trunk, took out our luggage, and started walking to the depot. I had no choice but to follow.

Thirty minutes later we were settled into our seats on the Metro-North, headed for Grand Central Station and the shuttle to La Guardia. From La

Guardia, we'd fly into Wilmington, North Carolina, where Julie would pick us up. Our plan was to stay with her for several days before making the trip by car down to my family in South Carolina.

Al promptly opened a newspaper, making it clear the subject of Carol was closed. But there was no way I was going to remain silent for the next ninety minutes.

"Al, what is really going on? I thought your relationship with her and all your other women ended years ago, or so you have led me to believe. You told me you were a changed man and that I could trust you again. And I have trusted you. Completely."

"Look, Maddie, there's no reason for you to be upset. I didn't talk to her just now. She doesn't know that I'm on vacation, nor does she need to know. I might tell her later if it comes up in a conversation. I don't tell her everything."

"Obviously. Because the woman doesn't even know we've been living together for the past five years. So what is it you're not telling *me* about your relationship with *her*?"

"Nothing," Al said, opening his newspaper again. "Because it's not important. It has nothing to do with us."

The man could sound so rational when he wanted to. But I wasn't buying it. My happiness had taken a drastic plunge. Just like the first time Al had blindsided me with another woman, I had not seen this deception coming. Only this time I didn't have a cup of coffee to toss at him.

Instead, I grabbed hold of his beard, turned his face to mine, looked him straight in the eyes, and said, "Let me be clear: I do not want her, or any other woman, in our life. Do you understand me? You and I have also been friends for a long time. And *our* friendship will not last if you continue to keep things from me."

"Let go, damn it," Al said, swatting at my hand. "Yes, I know we have a long history and I want it to continue."

"Then you need to be honest with us both. Tell her we're together and that you can't continue to see her."

Silence.

Obviously, we were going around in circles with this. In order to enjoy my trip home I'd have to try to let it go for now.

We left our New Haven home early and I had been sleepy, but now I was fully awake. Our long-awaited vacation was now under way. Our itinerary was filled with planned adventures and promising pleasures. My excitement had been building for weeks. Three years had passed since I had visited my family, and I was looking forward to seeing everyone. Our plans included attending a church homecoming in Little River, dinner with my cousin and sister, tours of the area, and hopefully a meet-up with Joan, another of my good friends from nursing school. I would have to find a way to put this behind me so that we could enjoy ourselves.

But I just kept thinking of Carol. I had never met her, but Al once told me that she was about ten years younger than he was, petite, pretty, with black hair and dark brown eyes. They had met in a group therapy class when their respective marriages were in trouble. Although Carol suffered from schizophrenia and regularly went off her meds, Al was attracted enough to initiate an affair between them, made even more titillating by the fact that Carol wrote erotic novels on the side. Carol's kinky sex helped boost his ego. Bragging with a smile on his face, Al said she made him feel like a stud muffin. He liked to boast about how sexually inventive she was. They were fond of acting out the kinky acts she described in her books. I doubt that they could assume those positions now. Anyway, he was too old for kinky sex.

But Carol was no longer a ghost from his past. She was an earthly person who was part of his present. Given their history, I had a hard time believing they were just friends. Now I began to imagine the worst: that they had reignited their affair.

My thoughts raced. When Al taught at Yale, he spent the night at his house in New Haven. I was never with him, opting instead to make the commute back to the village on weekends. His actions during the week were unknown to me. Had Al's time in New Haven aided him in leading a double life the entire time we had been living together? I couldn't recall a single incident before today that made me suspicious of him, but now I began to doubt myself. Had there been signs that I subconsciously ignored? Our previous relationship had fallen apart years ago due to his bad choices. Why did I think this time around would be any different? Our contract outlined an alliance similar to a marriage. Other women and men were not part of our deal. Obviously, Al had chosen to ignore that paragraph.

Then again, I chided myself, Al was much older now, no longer capable of swinging from chandeliers, so to speak. He would celebrate his seventy-first birthday next year. While still handsome, touches of gray now peppered the curly dark hair on his head and in his beard. His once toned body sported a slight paunch, and he was stiff when he got out of bed in the morning. Had he actually matured to the point where he *was* capable of just being friends with a woman? Al must have sensed that I was still spinning this in circles in my head, because he put down his paper, turned to me, and patted me on my thigh.

Al's characterization of this harlot type of woman showed that she was totally unlike me. We were and are as different as night and day. I was the type of woman he could have taken to meet his mother while Carol was the kind of woman to keep hidden under his bed from his mother! I did not want to believe all he had told me about their affair nor that he was in contact with her, but he admitted that he was. Since Al was being disrespectful to me by just talking to her in my presence, what was he doing behind my back? Hearing him talk and brag about his past lovers still made me angry. Al thought my jealousy and anger were funny. The situation was no laughing matter to me. He had never seen me in full-blown anger except when he admitted his planned marriage years before, and if he continued his current activities, he would surely hear and feel it. I was in a bad kettle of fish! His cell phone had rung out his secret life with another woman.

I did have questions, though. When did he resume interest in an old flame, and how long had it been going on? Would their past and new history haunt me now?

Al must have sensed that I was still spinning this problem in circles in my head, because he put down his paper, turned to me, and patted me on my thigh.

"Al," I said, "what a mess you have created! You know this will be your first visit with my family and friends. You know I have been excited about showing you off. Now I am uncertain of our relationship. I am no longer sure that traveling to my home with you is a good idea." My eyes were opened. I would wait and see how this developed, but for now my pride and trust in him were diminished. Was he deceiving me again? Time would tell.

"Nothing has changed, Maddie," he said softly. "So let's try and have a good time. You've told me so much about your family. Finally meeting everyone will be nice. Don't worry about the phone call. That should not mean anything to you. It certainly didn't to me."

I smiled weakly and nodded. Still, I couldn't help feeling we now had a third person riding with us down to North Carolina.

After arriving at LaGuardia, we checked in and went through airport security, walked to our terminal, and settled down to wait for our flight. Then Al said his legs were bothering him and he needed to take a walk. He also needed to go to the restroom again. He'd already been a couple times during the train trip, and once again when we got to La Guardia.

I looked at my watch. We had about twenty minutes before boarding. "Want me to go with you? I wouldn't mind getting a cup of coffee to take on the plane."

"No, no. I'll get it for you," Al said. "You stay here and get in line for us when they start to board."

Twenty minutes later he strolled up to where I was waiting to board the plane, his jacket flung casually over his left shoulder, held in place with his index finger hooked into the collar. It was what I called Al's peacock posture, one that said to the world, "Look at me, I'm virile and important." Of course, he'd forgotten my coffee.

"Al, are you all right?" I asked, trying not to use my nurse's voice.

"Oh, darn it! I forgot your coffee," he said. "Sorry. I can run back quickly if you'd like."

"No, it's not a big deal," I said. "I'm more worried about your frequent visits to the restroom and your aching legs. Are you feeling okay?" But to myself I wondered if his trips were excuses for something else.

Then I noticed his trousers were unzipped and part of his shirttail was hanging out. Pointing downward, I whispered to him, "Al, you really shouldn't try to multitask while using the urinal. Your phone is creating problems for you."

I was teasing more than I was serious, but Al's face turned bright red. Whether because his fly was unzipped or because he thought I thought he had returned Carol's call while he was in the bathroom, I don't know, and I didn't have time to ask. Holding back a laugh out loud, I wondered how long he had roamed the terminal, eying women, with his fly opened and his shirttail poking through. He did not look like a stud muffin to me or anyone important. As Al discreetly zipped his fly and tucked in his shirt, our line had begun to move.

Our flight to Wilmington was uneventful. We chatted, read magazines, and napped. Al didn't use the restroom once. His urinary problem must have resolved itself. As we began our descent, my excitement at seeing friends and family began to trump my worries about Carol. Soon we'd be on the ground, and I'd be enveloped in the warmth of my friends and family. Maybe I had been overreacting.

Chapter Six

JULIE MET US AT THE AIRPORT. Thank goodness she was in a happy mood. I needed a large dose of southern cheer. Unlike the rest of my friends and family, Julie had actually met Al. Initially reluctant given his past behavior, she finally agreed to visit us at Twin Oaks Manor a few years back. By the end of her three-day visit, she'd pronounced Al "charming." He seemed to like her, too.

"Welcome to Wilmington," she said once we were in her car. "I'm so glad y'all are here. I've been looking forward to your visit for months."

Julie was practically a member of my family, so we had a lot to catch up on. Al, who was sitting in the backseat, seemed amused by our enthusiastic conversation and on occasion asked me to translate something Julie said. "I guess I'm going to have to brush up on my Southern Belle speak," he said, making Julie blush.

Upon arriving at her home, we unloaded the car and Julie showed us to our accommodations, two guestrooms connected by a short hallway, each with an adjoining bath and each lovingly decorated with family heirlooms. Very often during my previous visits, Joan would make the trip down from her home in North Myrtle Beach, South Carolina. Over the years, one room had become known as Joan's room and the other as Maddie's room. "Y'all can choose whichever room you want to say in,"

Julie said brightly. "I know you are tired, so if you want separate bed-rooms you are welcome to them. They both have queen-sized beds. Large enough for your own space, but still . . . intimate. Everything is ready for you, but if you need anything, please let me know." She gave me a quick wink and left us to unpack.

Little did my friend know that intimacy was the furthest thing from my mind. The last thing I wanted was to touch Al or have him touch me. Privacy was what I craved, and this arrangement of rooms would give me what I needed, so we chose to be by ourselves.

Suddenly it occurred to me that perhaps I wasn't really Al's signifi-cant other. After this morning, I wasn't sure how long he would be mine, either. Very quickly, a major change had occurred in our relationship. One phone call is all it had taken. Too bad I hadn't known about Carol before now. I would have insisted that Al stay home, or I might not have gone on vacation at all. It would have been easier to sort all this out in the privacy of our own home. Now I could do nothing but put it on the backburner. That didn't mean I could fake an intimacy I didn't feel—not that Al and I were acting like the loving couple from just the day before. A distance had grown between us since that morning. For all his assur-ances during our trip, he had never once kissed me, never once held my hand. He'd seemed self-involved and dismissive, brightening only when we finally met up with Julie. A shade had been lowered on the window of my happiness, and I didn't know when or if I'd be able to raise it again.

Once unpacked, Al and I headed downstairs to find Julie in the kitchen, putting together a tray of snacks. I didn't want to settle in just yet. Outside, the weather was warm and sunny, the winds calm—great beach weather.

"Julie, can we wait to eat?" I asked. "The weather is so nice, I'd like to go for a swim. We might not get a chance tomorrow. I hear there's a front coming in." May was one of North Carolina's most unpredictable months, sunny and hot one day, the next cold and rainy, with intense thunderstorms.

Julie readily agreed, and we all headed off to our rooms to get our things. I thought Al might want to stay behind, but he seemed game as well. I was tempted to ask him not to go, but that would have seemed odd to Julie. I didn't have the energy to explain to her what had happened today, much less hear her say, "I told you so."

Within minutes we were back in the car headed to Wrightsville Beach, a two-square-mile resort island twelve miles from Wilmington. A few boats were cruising down the waterway. People were walking, running, or pushing baby strollers around the loop. Houses dotted the shoreline.

Luckily, we found a parking place at Johnnie Mercer's Pier. The original wooden pier weathered storm after storm until two hurricanes in 1996 destroyed it entirely. The new structure, reopened in 2002, was built entirely of concrete in order to withstand up to two-hundred-mile-per-hour winds. Extending twelve hundred feet out across the water, the pier remains one of the area's most popular landmarks and fishing spots. Julie herself had many fond memories of her time there as a teenager in the 1950s, and she shared a hilarious story of how her first kiss, with a boy who took her to the pier to fish, had nearly ended in disaster when he lost his footing and almost fell over backward into the water below.

Shoeless, we walked on the warm white sand and found a spot to spread our towels. Thankfully, there wasn't any competition for space. Most tourists had not yet arrived, so there were fewer people than there would be in a month.

I walked down to the water and found it warm enough for an ocean romp. "Come on in, you guys," I said.

Julie waved me off. "If you don't mind, I'll sit and read while y'all are swimming. I can come here anytime, and I don't feel like getting all wet and salty. I just want the sun. Enjoy yourselves, but be careful. The waves look rough."

I shrugged. "Maybe it will calm down soon," I said. "But I at least need to get some sun.

Al and I are as white as the bellies of the fish that swim in this ocean."

I spread my towel on the sand and removed my cover-up. As Al removed his T-shirt and Bermuda shorts, I saw with dismay that he was wearing an old Speedo suit. When I say old, I mean almost ratty. The fabric had gotten very thin. His legs were not only white, but they looked skinnier than ever beneath the bulge of his abdomen, which had been growing due to age and an increasingly sedentary lifestyle. Gone were the washboard abs of his youth, and there was gray sprinkled throughout his chest hair. I hadn't paid much attention to the changes in his body until now, but seeing him this way was alarming. The Speedo did nothing to enhance his appearance. Mentally, I chided myself. I was no spring chicken myself, and was just being critical because I was hurting. Growing old in a loving relationship meant that you accepted your partner's physical flaws and they yours. But that phone call had definitely caused a shift in how I felt about Al.

I noticed that Al was strutting, but who in the world was he trying to impress? Perhaps strutting was all he could do today. His sexual drive had waned, though he would never admit it. Even so, there weren't that many people on the beach, and I knew the preening wasn't for me. If he thought Julie cared about how he looked, he had another think coming. Al was not at all her type of man. With his scraggly beard and shaggy hair he looked like an aging hippie—definitely not the clean-shaven, elegant, southern-gent types whom Julie preferred. Al's suit was slightly baggy and it showed more of what he did not have than what he did. I became aware that Al had not worn a jockstrap. That meant little Johnny and the Twins—a nickname I'd come up with for Al's privates years ago—were hanging free. What a sight he made!

I glanced over at Julie. She, too, had noticed. Her eyes crinkled with mirth as she acknowledged my gaze, then covered her face with her book. She was trying hard not to laugh out loud, but I could see her shoulders shaking.

I couldn't hold my tongue, and I called out, "Al, why in the world are you wearing that old, worn-out suit? The new one I got you looks so much better on you."

By now Al was knee deep in the water. "Come on, Maddie. This old suit still looks good on me. Besides, it's comfortable."

"Al," I said, laughing, "it's not comfortable, it's worn out! That elastic looks gone. Watch out. If it falls off, the fish just might find something interesting to nibble on. I have heard of shrimp bait, worm bait, but never penis bait. So be careful out there."

Al just smiled and dove into the water. I knew he still thought of himself as a sexy young man. At our age, most people do not flaunt their bodies, sexy or not, and seeing him like this turned me off. And if Carol had seen him like this lately, then she needs glasses. He needed more than a tummy tuck. He needed a full body lift—and the genital equivalent of Miracle-Gro.

Even though friends would tell me that I still looked great in a bathing suit, for some reason that day I felt self-conscious. I have never been one to flaunt myself or even to wear a conservative two-piece suit, much less a bikini, but I had always felt good in my stylish one-pieces. Maybe it was seeing Al in his skimpy suit that made me question my own body. As with all women when we age, my body had changed, but it hadn't really bothered me. I had long accepted the fact that I was aging. And while my figure had filled out, my abdomen had remained flat and my arms firm— no chicken wings for me. Neither was I graying—my hair remained the same sun-streaked blond of my youth. Many people had considered me a beauty, but I always regarded myself as ordinary. I do take care of myself, however. I try to eat right and get plenty of exercise. Frankly, unless my mirror lies, I still look pretty darn good. But after seeing Al in his Speedo, I had to silently ask myself, *Do I actually look old and dowdy, too?*

Enough! I chided myself silently. *Sixty-two is not an old lady!* I was obsessing over things I usually never worried about, and mocking Al to boot. I had to decide: Would I let the phone call from Carol ruin my good time, or would I put this aside until we got home and I could deal with the subject privately? I decided then and there to try and have a good time.

After all, this was Al's first trip to the eastern shores of North Carolina. He had always loved swimming in the ocean and riding the large white-capped waves of the blue-green Atlantic waters, but this was his first swim in the southern Atlantic. The large waves crashed hard, loud, and foamy against the beach, a sign that the surf was getting rougher. Al was undaunted. "Come on in, I dare you," he called to me. "The water is fine. The waves are not as high or as hard as you might think. We can jump them together."

As he was talking a tall, tan, bikini-clad woman in her early twenties pranced along the beach in front of us. Al's eyes shifted from my face to her backside.

"No way," I called back. "Remember, I grew up on this coast and I have a deep respect for the power of its waves."

Al was so focused on watching the shapely young woman that he stopped paying attention to the water. Suddenly, a tall white-tipped gray wave rolled forth and knocked him down. The rough tide carried him to the shore. When he finally got his feet in the sand he stood up, water streaming from his beard and hair. He was sputtering and spitting salty water from his mouth and holding up the front of his Speedo with one hand. But the backside had fallen down, offering Julie and me a quick glimpse of his pale butt cheeks. His back was facing me, and his backside was fully exposed. Thank goodness little Johnny did not make a public debut! His skimpy suit had almost come off. He was not a pretty sight! Had he not been holding on to the suit it probably would have washed away. As events unfolded, I laughed out loud and didn't care if he heard me. The scantily clad woman had not even seemed to notice him in the water. Too bad the young woman had moved along, as she'd missed quite a show. Laughing, Al pulled up his suit as if nothing had happened and dove under another wave.

Chapter Seven

ONCE BACK HOME AT JULIE'S, we showered, dressed, and decided on an early-evening tour of historic Wilmington, followed by dinner. Traveling south on Market Street, we made our way downtown and parked on Water Street. Old live oak trees lined both sides of the street, their branches reaching out like arms to form a canopy over our heads. Wilmington is a port city located on the Cape Fear River in New Hanover County. During the Civil War it was a leading port for blockade-runners, and today it lures visitors from all over the world with its Old South history and charm. The three of us chatted while we strolled leisurely along the scenic riverwalk, admiring the majestic old homes that seemed to hold court over the water. We enjoyed browsing in the shops situated along the cobblestone streets.

Horse-drawn carriages made their way throughout the city with a *clip-clop* sound. A red trolley wound its way down the bumpy brick pavement, carrying sightseers. Smiling, we waved to the passengers, and they returned our greetings. More old oak trees, draped with Spanish moss that resembled a pirate's beard, swayed in the gentle breeze. The azalea blooms were dead and so were the dogwood blossoms, but other flowers and trees were blooming beautifully.

Suddenly nostalgic, I said to Al, "I wish you could have seen the azaleas at their full peak. It seems like yesterday when I was in high school and my friends and I would come up here for the Azalea Festival Parade. We felt so grownup. Those were fun times. Where have all the years gone?"

A lot had changed since I was a teenager, but many historical features remained just the same as I remembered them. "That tree over yonder has been there a long time," I said, my southern accent returning. "I have no idea how old it is, but I remember us resting in its shade." I hadn't lived in the South for over forty years—I'd left right after high school for college and never returned except to visit. But as the saying goes, you can take a girl out of the South, but you cannot take the South out of a girl. To me, that's a good thing. I'm proud of my roots.

But enough with the reminiscing. It was time for dinner. We chose the Pilot House, a favorite spot with locals and visitors alike. Situated right on the riverfront overlooking the water, the Pilot House served classic southern-style cooking with an emphasis on freshly caught seafood and shellfish dishes. The evening was balmy, with enough breezes to keep the mosquitoes and no-see-ums away, so we chose to eat outside on the waterfront under an umbrella-covered table. Our meal was presented beautifully, the food's quality and flavor exceptional. We could see why the restaurant had earned such a great reputation.

Dinner was relaxed and unrushed, and Al remarked on the beautiful views across Cape Fear, admiring both the hulking gray USS *North Carolina*, a World War II warship that was now a memorial, and the four-lane Cape Fear Memorial Drawbridge. As darkness progressed, car lights dotted the bridge, giving the appearance of Christmas lights strung along the sides. A riverboat cruised along the water, emitting a mournful blast of its foghorn.

Julie asked about Al's work, and he shared stories of his students and of his latest research. Al told current stories of his college professor life and what his children were up to. Al asked Julie how long she intended to keep nursing, and she laughed. Like me, she loved her work and hoped to be able to continue for a few more years at least.

Since Al claimed never to have enjoyed southern-style seafood, he had ordered prime rib. We teased him, saying he was missing out. North Carolina cooking was not to be missed. So he agreed to sample my shrimp, scallops, and oysters.

"Careful, Al," Julie said. "Oysters have a powerful effect on the libido."

"Is that so?" he replied, and winked at me. "Look out, Maddie! I might be chasing you round Julie's."

Al had always been a flirtatious and charming dinner companion, and I felt myself blushing in spite of myself. After all, it hadn't been that long ago when a dinner such as this, filled with good food, good drink, and good conversation, would have ended with us chasing each other amorously around the bedroom.

Then I brought myself back down to earth. Clearing my throat, I said, "Yes, well, I've heard that said about raw oysters, but I doubt it applies to fried."

"I don't know," Al said, trying to mimic my accent, "Y'all sure do fry just about everything down here."

That was certainly true. While we'll steam, bake, sauté, and grill our seafood, our all-time favorite way to eat it is fried to a golden brown. Ask any southern woman how to fry seafood, and she'll tell you to first melt a pound or more of lard in a big ol' cast-iron skillet, then drop the flour-dredged morsels in the hot fat, and cook until golden brown. Yum!

"And don't forget the hush puppies," I said, and then popped another one in my mouth. It was just as hush puppies should be: so light and airy they almost float, served with plenty of honey butter for dipping.

"Sure enough," Julie continued. "Y'all ever heard the expression the 'boardinghouse reach'? I think it was invented because of hush puppies. You gotta keep the basket filled at all times so you don't interrupt the conversation."

I laughed. "No watching the carbs, fat, and calories for me, at least not on this trip."

"Me neither," Julie agreed. "I can't think about how it will all look on my hips in a week or so. I'll be back at the gym, running my butt off."

How arteries stretch out to accommodate southern cooking is a medical mystery. Why, you can almost hear them saying, "Thank you, ma'am."

Dinner over, we strolled back up Market Street toward the car and discussed our plans for the next day, when Al and I would travel south to my hometown.

Once back at Julie's, we decided against a nightcap and opted instead to go directly to bed. Before heading upstairs, Al asked Julie if it was okay to open a window in his bedroom for some fresh air.

Julie shook her head. "My windows don't have screens, so insects will come in if you open them. Mosquitoes are out and about already. But there's a ceiling fan above the bed and the air conditioning is on. I'll lower the thermostat if you'd like."

The following morning at breakfast it was obvious that Al had not followed Julie's instructions. Bless his know-it-all heart, he had indeed opened a window. He was scratching at several areas on his arms and legs, and several times we noticed him putting his hand in his pockets to scratch the numerous bites on his private areas. Al sleeps in the nude, so the mosquitoes had made quite a feast of his skin. Little Johnny and the Twins must have been especially miserable!

Julie whispered to me, "Should I put a bottle of anti-itch cream in the bathroom?"

"Don't you dare," I replied. "He needs something to aggravate him."

Julie and I tried not to laugh as Al tried not to scratch. Maybe he had learned his lesson. Still smiling, we sat down to eat. Al squirmed a lot during the meal and scratched his not-so-private areas. Bless his heart, indeed!

We enjoyed a leisurely and relaxed continental-style breakfast in Julie's sunroom. She lives on a tidal creek, so the views are spectacular no matter the time of day. That morning we watched the sun dance on the water as it rippled in with the tide, listened to the squawk of seagulls, and watched beautiful wading birds feast on their own breakfast. After breakfast, we said our good-byes with a walk down to the dock and then headed back up to the house.

Over the years Julie and I had developed a tradition of sorts. Whenever I flew into Wilmington, she would pick me up, I'd spend a few nights with her, and then I'd pack up Baby, the old red Ford pickup she'd loan me for my use while visiting, and make the ninety-minute drive south to my hometown of Little River, South Carolina. This is when Julie would sometimes invite Joan and one or two other friends from nursing school for a mini-reunion. Each time we got together, we picked up our friendship right where we'd left off, as if no time at all had ever passed between visits. We proudly called ourselves GRITS, or Girls Raised in the South—and we had the T-shirts to prove it!

Naturally, Baby was at my disposal this time around. Al cast a skeptical eye at its vintage exterior, but I assured him the old pickup truck was as reliable as anything a rental car agency would charge us for. So with hugs all around and tears in my and Julie's eyes, Al and I set off. The plan for the next phase of our trip was to drive to Julie's second home, a condo in Ocean Drive in North Myrtle Beach, stay overnight, and then drive back across the Inland Waterway Bridge to Little River to see my family the next day.

Chapter Eight

ONCE WE BACKED OUT of Julie's driveway, Al asked me to find the nearest pharmacy. He needed some cream for his bites. I waited in the truck while he went inside and then to the restroom to apply the cream in private.

Back in the Ford I told Al how sorry I was that the insects had enjoyed such a bloodsucking ball the night before. "Between the fish and the mosquitoes, I bet there isn't much left of your Johnny," I said, switching to a teasing tone. "Not sure how you're going to operate with only a nub now. Here, let me see." I reached over as if to grab him.

Al jerked away like he had been shot, his mouth open in astonishment. "Since when is my misery laughable? It's not amusing to *me*, and I don't appreciate your tone."

"That's too bad, because I think the situation is funny as all get-out. That's what you get for thinking you know it all. Maybe next time you'll pay attention when someone gives you a warning."

In the past I had always laughed with him, not at him. But it was beginning to dawn on me that I had suppressed way too much of my natural jovial personality in an attempt to counterbalance Al's slightly immature boyishness. No more. As the days passed, Al would hear me laugh at him again, but he'd never see me cry.

We drove on in silence for the next few miles until we hit Ivy Cottage, a set of consignment stores that I often visited en route to my family. When I visit Julie this is always a stop that both of us look forward to and enjoy. Their merchandise is diverse, and the displays look professionally arranged. Al and I explored two of the cottages, and each of us came away with a small treasure that was easy to pack. He was also impressed with the antique and vintage wares. I purchased a beautiful piece of estate jewelry. Packing space was limited, and the old broach would not take up much space. Even Al purchased a seventeenth-century painting. After our purchases were complete we headed again for South Carolina and my old stomping grounds.

Al had never traveled in, much less driven, a pickup before. The closest he'd ever gotten to anything that size was his SUV. But despite having grown up partly in New York City, he always considered himself a country boy because he owns an estate and twelve acres in the Berkshires. When at home in Twin Oaks he would spend part of each morning walking in "his woods." He'd carry a long, self-made walking stick, imagining himself as king of his realm. As an only child, Al was spoiled by doting parents who continually told him how brilliant he was, how he'd grow up to be someone important. As a result he grew up into what many people considered an arrogant adult. That never bothered me because that was just Al. I admired what I considered to be his confidence.

When it came to his driving, rarely did I like to be in the car with him. He was a distracted driver, and I often wondered how much of his mind was on the traffic and weather and how much was elsewhere. Once he told me he'd crafted an entire lesson plan during a long commute, and during another he'd gotten the idea for a new sculpture. And, of course, I now wondered just how much time he also spent on the phone while in the car.

We were traveling on US 17, the long stretch of highway that runs close to the Atlantic coast from up north all the way down to its terminus in Punta Gorda, Florida. At one time Hwy 17 was called the king's highway because this was the route the British king's representative traveled to visit the colonies. Even now Hwy 17 Business, in Myrtle Beach, is called the King's Highway. Our goal for the day was Julie's condo in North Myrtle Beach, perhaps the most famous of the many seaside towns that make up the Grand Strand, a scenic stretch of virtually uninterrupted beach that extends sixty miles between the towns of Little River and Georgetown. But I wondered, given Al's tendency to space out while driving, if he was even paying attention to anything I was telling him regarding the history of the area.

Just then his cell phone rang. My heart lurched.

Al answered casually, listened to the voice at the other end, and then said, "Sorry, I'll have to call you back later. I can't talk now." Pause. "Yes, right. Again, I'll have to call you back, okay?" Then he clicked off the phone and turned to look out the window.

Gripping the steering wheel, I gathered up my courage and asked, "Al, do you think this trip was a good idea? Ever since learning about Carol, I've been feeling unsure about our situation. I don't know if I want to introduce you to my family and friends. I don't want you to embarrass me or talk to women on the phone while in the presence of my friends or family. I don't think I could explain it or make excuses for it."

"You worry too much," Al said, still looking out the window. "Our relationship is just fine. Of course I won't embarrass you. I've told you that the phone calls mean nothing."

"Maybe not. Still, perhaps you would prefer to stay in the condo or go to the beach to swim while I visit family and friends. If that's your decision, it will be fine with me."

"Let's continue to enjoy our vacation as we planned it. I have been looking forward to this. I don't want to spend all my time at the pool or in the ocean. I want to see the area. I might see something I'd like to paint or sculpt."

Oh, well. I had given him an option. I did not want my friends or family to sense my unease or to question our relationship. I would just have to make the best of the situation.

We were now leaving the coast and heading into farm country. Rows of newly planted crops lined the roadside. Some crops would be harvested this summer, while others would wait until fall. This region produced a wonderful variety of vegetables and was especially known for its strawberries, although that harvest was nearly over. As a former farm girl, I found the neat, straight, furrowed rows attractive and remembered the hard work it took to make them so. Al asked me about cotton and tobacco, although he'd see neither during this trip. I did tell him about the needle-sharp sand spurs that grew prolifically in the soil, explaining how painful they were when you stepped on them barefoot. The best way to remove them was with tweezers. Cockleburs were another nuisance that grew in the South. Since he had never seen one, I told him to imagine a miniature brown porcupine in the shape of an egg. I then recounted a practical joke we'd pulled as kids on unsuspecting guests. "We told people that the burrs were porcupine eggs, and if they slept on them they would hatch. Some people took us up on it and woke up with burrs in their butts. But most were pretty good-natured about it."

Al laughed. "Those folks must have been really gullible."

"So listen to me when I tell you to wear your shoes when you're outdoors, okay?"

Al rolled his eyes at me, but he was smiling when he did it.

Our weather was still cool back home in New England, but South Carolina felt unusually warm for May. Al suggested we hit the beach for a swim to cool off and get some exercise after an hour in the car. I checked the sky and could see dark clouds gathering in the distance. "If we hurry, maybe we can beat the storm," I said, and turned off onto Highway 9. My goal was to cross the Waterway Bridge to Sea Mountain Highway and then drive down to Cherry Grove Beach, a family-oriented oceanfront resort lined with the modern homes and high-rise condominiums that had long ago replaced the old-fashioned beach cottages of my youth.

Once at the pier, we used the public restrooms to change into our swimsuits. Thankfully, Al was wearing his new swim trunks, which looked so much better on him. There were more people on this beach than there had been at Wrightsville, and I would have been extremely embarrassed had Al chosen to strut his stuff in that ratty old Speedo.

But we had bigger problems than an ill-fitting pair of swim trunks. The sky had quickly grown even darker and the wind had picked up. The surf was churning, and it was much rougher than the day before at Wrightsville. Fishermen began quickly pulling in their lines and packing up their gear. Heeding their warning, we decided to take a quick walk on the beach instead of going for a swim. We had not gone far when the storm met us savagely. Thunder crackled in the distance, followed by loud booms of thunder that increased in volume as the storm quickly made its way inland. These sudden, violent storms were typical of South Carolina in a dry, hot summer, but rare in spring, when storms brought gentle rains without all the drama. I had never been comfortable with storms, especially thunderstorms, and as a child would hide inside my bedroom closet until they passed. Out here, though, there was nowhere to hide.

Then the rain started, a heavy, pewter-colored curtain of moisture that hung over the water until you couldn't tell the clouds from the ocean. Everyone along the pier and shore made a dash for cover. We could barely see ahead of ourselves as we tried to follow the crowd to shelter. The feeling was downright spooky. Then Al grabbed my hand and pulled me under the pier—I hadn't even seen it, the wind and rain were whipping so forcefully. We weren't safe from the lightning, but at least we were under heavy cover. We had left our umbrellas in the pickup, so had no choice but to wait out the storm. Most likely they wouldn't have done us much good anyway. We watched as some people tried to pop theirs, only to lose them to the force of the wind. We weren't alone under the pier, and we caught bits and pieces of conversation about the sudden downpour. "Where did that storm come from?" "Did you see how quickly the sky turned almost black?" "I haven't see rain this hard in a long time." "Are we safe under here?" "Looks like we won't be able to fish today." "I hope no one got caught out in a boat."

Once the rain began to slacken, we sprinted for the truck.

"Well, that was exciting," Al said, drying his hair and beard with his beach towel. "And I've worked up an appetite. Is there a sandwich shop nearby where we—" His voice was cut off by the noise of a sudden cloudburst, the rain pounding out a staccato symphony against the truck's windshield and roof. Once again, we'd have to wait out the storm. Our abating adrenal rush, coupled with the fact that we hadn't eaten since breakfast, was making us both drowsy.

To try and stay awake, I said in a voice loud enough to be heard over the rain, "At least the rain will bring beautiful May flowers. And everyone's lawns will begin greening."

Al took his towel and tried to wipe the condensation from the inside of the windshield. "I think this is the heaviest rainstorm I have ever seen. I can't believe the amount of water that's coming down."

"Since we're just a few feet above sea level, the rain will soon run into the ocean or be absorbed quickly by the sand," I said. "No possibility of flooding, at least. Speaking of which, I often wonder if the biblical flood began with rain this hard. If we had rain for forty days and forty nights we probably *would* flood, and we'd have to find something to float in. Just imagine what that would be like."

Al laughed. "Madeline, I swear, you think the strangest things at times."

Soon enough the rain slackened to a drizzle and we were able to head out. We decided to forgo stopping at a diner and instead we picked up a six-pack of Pepsi and some snack crackers—referred to in the south as nabs— at a local convenience store so we could get back on the beach for a walk. I couldn't convince Al that we should also pick up a bag of peanuts to add to the Pepsi. He'd never heard of such a thing, but I assured him it had been one of my favorite treats as a child. In fact, I said, anyone who'd never tried it was downright deprived. The only thing missing from this particular trip down memory lane was a Moon Pie, but unfortunately the store didn't carry them.

By the time we finished buying our snacks, it was still drizzling but the sky was beginning to clear. Barefoot and holding our shoes, we went walking on the beach. Thinking about my childhood, I realized just how lucky I'd been to grow up both on a farm and this close to the ocean. It was important to me to share those memories with Al, just as he had shared memories of his own youth with me.

As a first-generation German American born to immigrant parents who made the trek to the United States from Cologne, Al grew up speaking German. His full name is Albert. Most of his friends and family grew up calling him Bert, but I've always called him Al. It's how he introduced himself to me. His last name, Falk, means falcon in German. Al had lived a much more leisurely life as a child than I. The New York City of his youth was a much different place than it is today. Children could play on neighborhood streets safely and ride their bikes without incident throughout much of the city. He and his family spent their summers at Twin Oaks Manor, where Al, an only child, rode horses and explored the surrounding woods. In addition, he also attended camps for artists and musicians. It's not surprising that he couldn't fathom my life on the farm, where my family raised tobacco.

"In those days," I told Al, "it seemed that thunderstorms, like the one we are now experiencing, always came during the heat of the summer and in the afternoons, right when we were working in the fields. We could smell the ozone in the air, and the leaves on our oak trees would turn inside out when the wind began to stir."

The storms were as frightening then as they are today, I explained, and we'd have to move quickly to barn the harvested tobacco when the weather got nasty. During the tobacco harvest, my brother and some of our employees worked in the fields, pulling the golden yellow leaves off the tall green stalks. Tobacco usually ripens from the bottom up, so harvesting the leaves requires a lot of bending. At times, it felt as if you were trying to stand on your head. Green leaves were left on the stalks to be "primed" when they had ripened.

At even the most distant clap of thunder, my brother, who drove the International Harvester tractor with a trailer attached, would yell to everyone to climb aboard, and he'd drive them as quickly as possible to the barn, bumping along the dirt rows, everyone holding on for dear life. A lightning strike could have killed any of them at any second. You can bet that the women, who worked under a shelter, breathed a sigh of relief when the men finally gathered inside with them. A few of the boys tried to make light of the situation, but deep down, everyone was scared. Lightning was nothing to joke about.

Al just shook his head. "I can't imagine growing up like that. That sounds like an incredible amount of hard work."

I just shrugged. "It was. Raising tobacco is nonstop hard work from dawn to dusk, and even sometimes into the night when the tobacco is curing. But sometimes it can be fun. We were a close-knit family, and our workers were like family, too. Farm work gave me a physical and mental strength that has stayed with me throughout my life."

But while I never regretted growing up on a farm, I did not want to spend the remainder of my life on one, either. I am thankful that it taught me the value of hard work and built character, but my plan ever since I entered high school was to grow up and become a nurse.

Despite the light rain, our walk had been pleasurable and my reminiscing fun. There had not been any more phone calls either, so I even began to think that I had blown things out of proportion.

Chapter Nine

By THE TIME WE MADE IT back to Baby, the sun was almost fully out, even though the streets remained slick with rain. I decided to give Al a leisurely tour of Ocean Boulevard, one of the most scenic streets along the Grand Strand. Those people who think the South is mostly rural and poverty-ridden would be astonished at the mansions that line the beach here.

"Wow," he said, his neck craning to take in the splendid homes, "who would have guessed at all this wealth? Is Julie's place like any of these?"

I shook my head and told him that her townhome in North Myrtle Beach, also in Ocean Drive, was much more modest, but nice nonetheless. On our way there, I pointed out various sights. So much had changed over the years. The gated community of Seaside Plantation was once Gator Hole Golf Course, while Robbers Roost Golf Club was now a housing development and a shopping center. All the streets were paved. I drove by some of the schools that I had attended. Vanna White, who was born in Conway and raised in North Myrtle Beach, had attended many of these same schools as well. Al didn't particularly care about all this, but I was enjoying this trip down memory lane.

After arriving at Julie's, we showered and changed into dry clothes. Al and I opened up her house and unpacked our belongings. It was dark by the time we arrived back from an early dinner and grocery shopping, but the rain that had started up again just after our arrival had stopped. The lower temperatures made the night perfect for a walk in nearby McLean Park.

The evening was beautiful, and it should have been romantic as well. The park was ringed with myrtle and oak trees dripping with Spanish moss, their shadows making lacy gray patterns against the grass. The air was full of sound: the quiet rustling of birds as they settled down for the night, male crickets chirping their mating calls, the occasional croak of a bullfrog. Ducks glided over the lake with their ducklings in tow. The playground was empty—the children had long returned home for dinner and bed—but a few people were playing tennis, their balls making muted smacking sounds as they hit the racquets. Normally, Al and I would have walked hand in hand or stopped to cuddle for a bit on a nearby bench. But now that the day's excitement was over, I felt myself sinking into a gloomy mood. Al was silent as well, seemingly lost in thoughts he didn't want to share, and I wondered if he was enjoying himself. He had yet to say so. Neither of us attempted to engage in conversation. Something was definitely amiss.

"Al," I said, sadly, "what's wrong? Neither of us seems happy. We don't even want to talk to each other."

Al merely grunted and said, "Nothing is wrong with me. We've had a full day, and I'm tired is all. I could have gone to sleep in the pickup. It will feel good to hit the sack."

Al made a good point: it *had* been an exhausting day. And his phone had gone off only once. I put my doubts away for the time being, and we headed back to the townhouse.

Once back at Julie's, we both admitted that the walk had reenergized us and we weren't quite ready for bed. "How about a movie?" Al asked, squinting at the couple dozen DVDs on the bookshelf. "You pick."

I pulled a title that looked interesting and handed it to Al. Just as he was getting ready to load it into the machine, his phone rang. Whoever was at the other end of the line was doing most of the talking—and doing it loudly. It sounded like a woman to me. Al was smiling. In fact, he looked happier than I'd seen him the entire trip. After a couple minutes, he said, "That all sounds very interesting. Let me call you back in a few minutes, though, okay?"

I couldn't contain my anger any longer. "Which woman was that?" I spat out. "Is she another one that isn't important?"

Al shrugged and excused himself to go upstairs to use the restroom. I knew he was making a phone call.

When Al returned downstairs, I said, "Now I understand the reason for all your trips to the bathroom on the train and at the airport, for all those walks alone at Julie's to 'get some air.' You were actually making phone calls that you didn't want me to hear."

"Sure, I've returned a couple phone calls. I'm a busy man, and sometimes I have to conduct business on the phone."

"That's a crock, Al. And your timing couldn't be worse. Or maybe you wanted me to find out about your other life during our time together when I couldn't or wouldn't do anything about it."

"Wait a minute, Maddie. Don't blame me for your unhappiness. The phone conversations have nothing to do with you. Don't pay any attention to them and don't let them upset you. Please stop lecturing me about my phone."

"Al, please don't make me sound like I'm paranoid. Put yourself in my place. You would feel differently if I was the one ignoring you but acting happy around other people."

Before he could answer me, his phone rang again. As I listened to his side of the conversation, it became obvious that Al was also lying to the woman at the other end of the line. I was seeing a side of Al that I had not seen in years. I never thought he had lied to me about anyone since we had begun our lives together five years ago, but he certainly was lying and deceiving two people now.

How could I have been so blind? So stupid?

Once he hung up, I launched into him again. "Al, your behavior disgusts me. You are not the person I was looking forward to being with. I did not sign up for this kind of life when I agreed to live and grow old with you. Why don't you just return to Connecticut? You would have a much better time there."

"I'm not going anywhere," Al said. "Let's finish this vacation. I for one am having a good time."

"Well, then act like it," I said, then silently reprimanded myself for not having the guts to just kick him out.

But there was still a small part of me that desperately wanted Al to be telling me the truth. Was I that much in love with him, or was I that scared of being alone again? I tried to untangle my thoughts and think clearly. What *would* it mean if I left Al? Selling my house had been a huge mistake, but at least most of that money was still in savings and investments. That was a comforting thought. I might soon be homeless, but I was not destitute.

Feeling defeated and betrayed, I left Al with the movie and went upstairs to bed. I just wanted to get through the week as peacefully as I could. We would discuss our future, or lack thereof, once back home.

Having slept only a couple hours, I woke early the next morning and walked across the boulevard to the ocean to take photographs of the sunrise. The new day was beautiful, and the sky was clear. There was no sign of the storm from the day before. The vibrant sunrise was the perfect antidote to a tortured night spent thinking about Al's other woman. The peaceful time alone was just what I needed. I sat in the sand with my camera and watched the morning unfold while I snapped photo after photo of the water and the changing skies. Before returning to the townhouse, I roamed the beach looking for shells and sea glass.

Al wasn't far from my thoughts, though. Walking the shore, turning the trip's events over and over like a movie in my mind, I had to finally admit that the love of my life was an asshole. I smiled. The word would have earned me a good mouth-washing, as my parents had taught us children that dirty language shows poor breeding and a lack of education. My mama only had to use soap a couple times before we got the message. But in this case, Mama likely would have forgiven me. There was no other word to describe Al at this point.

But I had a bigger problem on my hands. There I was, sixty-one years old, an accomplished professional who had lived a happily independent single lifestyle in the thirty-some years between the time I divorced my first husband and the time I moved in with Al. So why was I putting up with his crap? Was I afraid of losing him because I truly loved him and believed our relationship could work, or was I just scared of the rejection and of being alone?

I knew I needed to make plans to leave, but on the other hand a small part of me was not ready for the end. Maybe once we were back home, Al would be able to more clearly see my point of view, honor my wishes, and stop seeing Carol. I had enough experience with mental illness to know that if she wasn't taking medication, she might be prone to the kind of manipulative drama that could cause irreparable damage to my life with Al. It was a terrible position to be in. Like an ostrich with its head in the sand, some might say. Only once I pulled it out, my eyes would still be filled with sand and the picture would still be grainy.

For now, however, I had to continue a semblance of a relationship until this trip was over. Then I would begin to think about what I should do and where I should go.

As was his custom, Al woke late and declined breakfast except for coffee. I made a cup of tea and joined him.

"Where did you go this morning?" Al asked.

"Down to the beach. The sunrise was absolutely stunning."

I leaned over to give him my camera and he scrolled through the photos one by one, making the occasional thoughtful comment.

"These are great," he said, handing the camera back to me. "You have always been an amazing photographer."

I felt my face flush from the unexpected compliment and my anger thawed just a bit. "So, the plan for the day is to attend my homecoming at my old church. Do you still want to go?"

"Fine with me," he replied.

"Okay, let's shower and change clothes. And leave a little early because I want to stop on the way up and pick up a pie and rolls. It would be impolite to go empty-handed."

Quickly Al ascended the stairs. He seemed almost chipper.

Chapter Ten

M y PLAN WAS TO TOUR my hometown for a bit before going to the church social. Legend has it that thanks to its position on the river of the same name, Little River was once a hideout for infamous pirates like Stede Bonnet and Blackbeard, and later on, bootleggers. Shops, galleries, cafés, businesses, and churches grace the streets. Many of my friends and family members still live in the area, and they are, like South Carolinians on the whole, the salt of the earth, with loving hearts and active minds. I was glad to be home.

Our first stop was the spot where I was born and raised. I grew up on a farm that had been in my family for generations. Before that, Waccamaw Indians lived and roamed on the land. We found many arrowheads and pottery shards over the years there, as well as seashells and sharks' teeth. My love of Native American lore began as a child and continues to this day.

Our land faced the highway, or "road," as we called it in those days. Our large two-story house was old and charming, nowhere near antebellum in style but still stately. We didn't have air-conditioning, but the massive old oak and pecan trees that graced the yard blocked the sun and kept the house cool during the summer's heat and humidity. Farming tobacco was a year-round, labor-intensive proposition for our family and other farmers.

Since we didn't live far from the river, it became one of our primary sources of entertainment on our rare days off from school or work. We swam in its clear waters, canoed its length for miles, and drifted in the rowboat, lazily watching the clouds form various pictures in the sky. My brothers would ride their bikes to the water to fish and from there would take home their day's catch for our mother to cook. The ocean was another of our playgrounds. I guess I grew up waterlogged and have never recovered. Although the northern East Coast would be my home as an adult, I returned to this area time and again.

Our farm is now home to a condominium housing development. The residents like to say that they live on a lake, which I find funny because growing up we called it our pond. We fished and watered our livestock there. I guess it sounds more upscale to say one lives on a lake rather than a pond, though, but it still made me laugh when I read the promotional brochure. I pointed out to Al exactly where our house stood, where the outbuildings were, where my mother grew her garden. I could also make out the gully, or swash, that ran along one edge of the farm. Once, lovely short-stemmed wild roses bloomed all summer long along its banks. The profusion of pale pink blossoms was beautiful to behold. Blue morning glories twined along a pasture fence and four-o'clocks grew by the barn. I remember checking to see if they really did open or close at four o'clock. Blackberry brambles also grew wild on the land. We children would pick the tart berries and take them home to our mother to make pies. Like Uncle Remus's Br'er Rabbit, we didn't want to land in the briar patch. Getting our clothes caught on the thorns was painful enough. In the woods, wild honeysuckle and wisteria vines climbed the trees and emitted a wonderful smell when in bloom. My brother Don and I used to swing on the thicker, sturdier stalks, pretending that we were Tarzan and Jane. Don tried and tried to get Johnny Weissmuller's Tarzan yell right but never managed it exactly. He beat on his chest with his fists and yelled anyway.

On weekends in summer we held oyster roasts and clambakes with watermelon and homemade ice cream; in the fall we organized hayrides, followed by hotdog and marshmallow roasts. Occasionally we kids would be allowed to go to the movies on Saturday night. Sunday mornings we spent in church, followed by noon lunch around the big family table heaped high with delicious food prepared by my mother and grandmother. My mouth still waters at the thought of her fried chicken, homemade biscuits, and sweet iced tea.

I didn't particularly care if Al could relate to my childhood memories or to life, past and present, in South Carolina in general. I shared them with him anyway because it did me good to reminisce. For today, at least, I could escape into my memories, one memory leading to another.

After our tour of where my childhood home was, we headed over to the church for the homecoming celebration. The old Protestant church and cemetery, set under a small copse of trees, was a special place for my family, and the center of our social as well as spiritual lives.

We arrived just after midday, but the festivities were already well under way. Children were running wild with excitement, playing hide-and-seek and kicking soccer balls. One of the adults, likely envisioning a ball landing in the middle of a bowl of potato salad, hollered in their general direction to "move y'all's game away from the food," before turning to the table to pile her plate high with fried chicken, mashed potatoes, and biscuits.

Al and I added our offerings to the table. "You want to grab a plate and eat before I start introducing you around?" I asked Al.

He shrugged, looking uncomfortable.

I handed him a sweet corn muffin. "Here, eat this. Maybe it will whet your appetite and make you less grumpy."

He did not appreciate my attempt at humor. "Maddie, I can tell I'm going to have nothing in common with these people. I have never been to a church's homecoming. My family didn't attend church regularly. Our idea of a party was completely different than this."

"True, we don't have a quartet playing for your entertainment," I said, smiling sweetly. "Just be glad this isn't a hog-killing affair. On second thought, chitlins might be just the thing for you." Unfortunately, my dig about cooked pig intestines went right over his head. I realized that he had no idea what they were.

Well, if he wanted to stay hungry and grumpy, that was his business. I had friends and family to catch up with. We southerners are an affectionate bunch, so I spent the next hour or so hugging and chatting with cousins and people with whom I'd kept in contact since high school. I introduced each of them to Al, who looked like he wanted to be anywhere but here. He could barely grunt out a cursory, "Hello, nice to meet you," much less engage anyone in conversation. At one point I heard him sigh with exasperation and mumble something in German. Imagine Al's surprise when he realized my good friend James, who teaches German at the University of South Carolina in Columbia, had understood every word of the comment, which was something along the lines of "damn country people and their picnics."

"Sir, I'm not sure what you're implying," James said to Al, as polite as could be. "I too am a southern country gentleman and happen to enjoy the gathering of friends and family. Dr. Falk, you are an arrogant, stupid ass. Because we speak with a different accent doesn't mean that we're stupid and uneducated.'

Al blushed, but didn't reply.

"Should I take that as a no?" James prodded. "Because I wouldn't want you to be in the position of having to defend your lack of intelligence, much less manners."

I smiled at my friend and mouthed a word of thanks. Then I turned to Al and whispered, "Please stop acting like a jerk and try to keep your rude mouth shut. You're embarrassing me. You left a book in the truck. Why don't you get it and sit under a tree or sit in the church and read? That should keep you out of trouble. Reading will be rude but not as rude as you insulting the people gathered here."

Just then, another friend of mine, whom I had dated briefly in high school, waved at me and started to walk over.

"Hey there, Maddie. Did you drive over here in that big ol' red truck again?"

Over the years I have always enjoyed driving Julie's truck to various outings with friends and family. People do double takes at the sight of me behind the wheel of the bright red Ford Ranger, it's just so unlike me.

"Hey, Richard," I said, giving him a hug. "You bet I did. I like to arrive in style."

"Hah, I knew it! I just love a good-looking, truck-driving woman," Richard said, giving me a huge smile.

That was the best thing about coming home: I could be who I truly was with these people. We could flirt and tease and laugh, and just let loose and have fun. I didn't have to watch what I said or did, like I often did around Al.

I thoroughly enjoyed the attention I received from Richard and the dozens of other people who sought me out. Their comments showed Al that I had people in my life who valued me and who treasured our friendship. Everyone seemed delighted that I had returned home to participate in the local gathering. For once, I was not concerned with how Al was feeling. As a result, I thoroughly enjoyed myself, basking in the warmth and love that radiated from these wonderful people. It had been a great day, regardless of Al.

Gradually, the picnic wound down and we all went our separate ways. Once back in the truck, Al sighed deeply and said, "Well, I have to admit it. That was so far my least favorite thing about this trip. I don't want to ever attend another 'homecoming,' so please don't invite me to one."

"Well, you weren't exactly Mr. Friendly, Al," I said. "Maybe if you'd just made an effort, but no, you had to be an arrogant ass. And don't worry about future picnics. I don't plan to invite you to another one—or on another vacation, either."

In typical Al fashion, he ignored my comment and instead made another dig. "You surely were popular with the men. You must have been a big flirt when you were a teenager."

"Oh, Al, if only you knew. Yes, I had a lot of fun as a teenager. A big group of us hung out together, but not a single one of us ever did anything scandalous or troublesome. The things we did were never an embarrassment, and we tried to make our parents proud. Many of our activities were centered around the church. We simply had good clean fun."

I have to admit it, though, I got a kick out of his jealousy. It restored my confidence. Seems Al hadn't expected that I'd been so popular and that men would flirt with me. For once, he hadn't been the center of attention. Knowing southerners as I do, I imagine they said of his arrogance, "He's not from around here, is he? Bless his heart." These gentle people would never want to hurt his feelings by saying more than that in public. However, in private they would say what a rude jerk he was, *bless his heart.*

Although we had plans for the evening, the remainder of the afternoon was ours. The problem was, did I want to spend it with or without Al? Arrogant jerk or not, we were still tethered to each other for the remainder of the trip, which included dinner that evening with my cousin Frank and sister Betty, who was driving up from Charleston. Betty, a high school English teacher, was married with two teenage boys, but they had a soccer game the next day so opted to stay home.

"Al," I said, taking the bull by the horns, "I'd like to spend the rest of the day by the water. You can come with me, or I can drop you back at the condo and go by myself."

"No, I wouldn't mind a good walk along the beach. All that standing around made me stiff."

"And what about tonight?" I asked, hoping Al would beg off dinner with my family. But, no, for some reason he seemed determined to believe that things were still status quo between us: just Maddie and Al, on vacation as usual.

College had ended for the semester, and the day was warmer and sunnier than it had been the day before, so the beach was bustling. Students wearing bathing suits were playing volleyball along the shore. Some were surfing. It was great to hear their happy shouts. Al could have gone for another swim, but he wasn't interested.

A band was playing on the pavilion, reminding me of my own time as a as a teenager dancing the "Carolina dance," later called the "shag," a dance similar in style to the jitterbug but of entirely southeastern roots. We danced to what is now called beach music. In fact, SOS ("Society of Stranders") Week is still hugely popular along the Strand, with junior shaggers carrying on the tradition of their parents and grandparents. Had I been feeling more loving toward Al, I would have grabbed him for a dance or two. And had I not been so stuffed from the church picnic, I would have bought a hot dog from one of the half-dozen vendors that lined the boardwalk. The smell of onions, chili, and wieners wafted through the air, another fond memory from my childhood. If I could figure out how to bottle or make a candle out of that aroma, I could make a fortune selling it.

Al was silent for most of our stroll, but I didn't mind. I was happy in my reverie, reminiscing about old times and thinking fondly of the warm welcome I had enjoyed at the picnic. It began to occur to me that my life did not revolve entirely around Al. There were people in this world that not only loved and valued me but who were open and honest with me as well.

Chapter Eleven

T HAT EVENING WE PULLED UP at my cousin Frank's home. He greeted us at the door with a big smile and hugs all around. Frank welcomed Al into the living room, asking him what he preferred to drink, while I checked in on Betty in the kitchen. Frank's wife, Doreen, was away at a church conference, a big disappointment for me since she and I were very close. Before she left, Doreen had premade our dinner and stuck it in the freezer, leaving Frank with detailed instructions on how to thaw each container and heat it up—which basically meant my sister was in charge.

After Betty and I made sure everything but the bread was in the oven, we poured ourselves some iced tea and joined the men in the living room. Like Al, Frank was a retired air force colonel. Both were commissioned officers. In spite of the age difference—Frank was my age—the men did have a lot in common and seemed to enjoy sharing military stories.

Frank had been stationed at Myrtle Beach Air Force Base until the government closed it, precipitating his move to Fayetteville, North Carolina, where he was stationed at the Pope Field air force base. After his retirement, he moved back to the area.

I knew Al had been in the air force, but he rarely mentioned those days to me. Now, however, with a kindred spirit of sorts to speak with, he began to share stories of his time in the service. During dinner, Al told the tale of joining a civilian flying club while he was stationed at Lackland Air Force Base in Texas. Because he was a military colonel, he was made team leader of the group. Turns out it was a mistake that nearly turned disastrous. On their long flight they got lost, and it was only by sheer luck that Al had navigated the crew back to base. Needless to say, none of the club members ever wanted to fly with him again.

Al, however, seemed to find the story amusing. "It was almost impossible to tell where we were from the air using a map and ground landmarks. I was perspiring heavily by the time we touched down. I decided before I landed that I didn't want to ever do that again!"

Al went on to explain that he jumped at the chance to transfer to Arizona. "I wanted to paint desert scenes, especially those around Sedona." Turns out, he started charming some of the local gals into posing nude for him as well.

"Oh, Al," I said, a hint of disgust in my voice.

"What?" he responded defensively. "The human form is one of the most difficult things to paint. I wanted to master it."

I rolled my eyes.

"Unfortunately, the general wasn't so enlightened," Al continued. "He invited me for a drink and then promptly presented me with my discharge papers."

Al laughed uproariously, but the rest of us were silent. I caught my cousin giving my sister a knowing look. *What must they think*, I wondered, *about this man who treated his service so casually?* All these tales happened years ago, long before I met him, but I was still embarrassed. My family must have questioned the kind of man with whom I had chosen to associate.

"So," Betty asked, ever the polite hostess, "what did you do after that?"

Al went on to explain that he entered graduate school at Yale. He was also granted an assistantship, which meant teaching a beginning-level art history course.

"I also spent the following five years teaching and studying sculpture, with a focus on the female figure," he added.

I broke into the conversation and couldn't seem to keep myself from saying, "Obviously, Al has had a long interest in studying female bodies."

My sister gave me one of her wide-eyed looks, but Al ignored me, intent on continuing his self-aggrandizing tale. This was the mid-1960s, and Al became enamored of the hippie movement, growing his hair long, wearing a peace sign necklace, beads, and tie-dyed shirts. Perhaps he was rebelling from the military image and his straitlaced youth. "Man, Yale was stuffy in those days," he said. "I certainly didn't look like a traditional Ivy League professor, that's for sure. The dean called me into his office several times, but I ignored their pleas to wear a suit and a tie. And I have yet to wear one. I was a good instructor, so they never could justify firing me. Been there ever since. The hippie and peace movements were over, but I didn't care that my looks did not convey the professionalism of an Ivy League professor. I thought I looked 'out of sight.'"

It's true that Al has always marched to the beat of his own drum, and could care less what anyone thinks of how he looks. Although he's long given up the tie-dye and love beads, he has always worn his hair long and always had a beard. I guess it's his way of sticking it to the man, a symbolic middle finger to the staid conventions of East Coast academia.

But I could tell that Frank and Betty were not amused. They had been raised to believe in the value of certain traditions, in societal order, and in dressing well as a sign of respect for one's vocation.

I was relieved when Al finally changed the topic and asked Betty about her work.

"I teach English at one of the high schools in Charleston. Students are not of the same temperament as we were growing up. Many people say that the school is like a war zone now."

"And you, Frank, what do you do?"

Frank explained that he was semiretired and worked part-time for a security company.

"Doreen's the main breadwinner now, huh?" Al said, winking. "How long you been married?"

"Doreen and I have been married for twenty-five years. Doreen does work at our church part-time. Both of us are breadwinners," Frank said irritatedly. "Our lives are not as colorful as yours, that's for sure."

Turns out, I learned during the ensuing conversation, that my cousin and Al also had a similar personal life. Doreen is Frank's second wife, and he has children and grandchildren from his first marriage. Al shared that he has a stepdaughter, a daughter, and a grandson, all by his *third* marriage. He said it as if he was embarrassed. "I know that I don't look old enough to be a grandfather, but I am. I have a cute little grandson. He looks like me when I was younger, without a beard, of course. Frank looked at me as if to say *what is wrong with this fellow?* I simply rolled my eyes. I had thought that Al had only been married once, to Joyce. Turns out that he had been married twice before, which was news to me.

I was glad that we had finished dinner, otherwise I might have choked on my food. I hid my shock by helping Betty clear the table.

Unfortunately, we still had dessert to get through—and Al was still in the mood to talk.

"I guess I would say my first marriage had been more about lust than love," he said. "I'd met a young woman who was pretty, shapely, and lavished me with a lot of attention in and out of bed. Like a spider, she spun her web and captured me in it. When my interest in her waned she faked a pregnancy and told me the child was mine, so I married her. I was doing what I thought was the right thing to do. Shortly thereafter, I had the marriage annulled when I realized she was not pregnant. I have never heard from her again. I don't really count that marriage. Frank, you must have known or heard of women who play this kind of game."

Frank cleared his throat. "Yes, but I've never been involved with one. Maybe my internal radar has been better than yours."

And now I had allowed Al to spin me in his web—only breaking those bonds would not be easy, and we were not even married. Had I insisted, at least I'd leave with alimony. He was *still* paying Joyce. When I did leave him, I would go as I had come, with just my belongings.

Another thought struck me. If Al had considered his first marriage a hoax, what did he consider his life with me? How would he describe our relationship at some future dinner, when some unsuspecting guest asked about the women in his life? That gave me something to seriously think about.

"And your second wife?" Betty asked. I shot her a look and she shrugged, as if to say, "He's only going to tell us anyway."

"I met my second wife while in graduate school at Yale. We had a whirlwind affair that led to marriage. I absolutely adored her. I thought we were compatible in every way, but she couldn't adjust to my schedule. Because of the demands of my job, I didn't have as much time to spend with her as she needed. That was a big mistake. She had an affair and ended up divorcing me. I was devastated, and it took me a long time to recover from the hurt because I deeply loved that beautiful woman. It's sad to even think about, but I heard she was killed in a car accident about six or seven years ago, I had not seen or heard from her in years."

We sat there listening and didn't know what to say. A wave of sadness came over me. Perhaps she was the only woman Al had ever truly loved. He only married Joyce out of obligation. But what had been his motivation with me? He had never once told me he absolutely adored me, much less that he loved me. I'd accepted that perhaps his practical German upbringing made him incapable of expressing grand passion. It was enough that he liked, respected, and admired me. It was enough on which to build an easy, noncomplicated life, but obviously not enough to keep him from his carnal pursuits.

Listening to Al, I realized that had he and I married as originally planned twenty-five years before, we might have also divorced. I would have been wife number four—or three, if, like Al, you don't count his first marriage. It hurt to know that I wasn't the only woman in Al's life, or, failing that, at least not his great love. Al was like a magnet, and I had a difficult time resisting his force. I do not know if it was fatal attraction, but it was certainly mentally and emotionally destructive.

I just sat there and said nothing when Al began to talk about Joyce, never once mentioning me. Even worse, I learned that Al had taken Joyce and her daughter on a three-week pre-honeymoon trip to France—the very trip he had promised we would take.

Betty stopped him from going further. She, unlike Frank, knew that Al had proposed to me before discovering that Joyce was pregnant and that he'd broken off our engagement because of it. "Well, now," she said, "that's all in the past. You have Maddie now. She told me all about the renovations you did on the family home. Sounds like you have a wonderful place to build your future together."

Al just smiled at her stiffly, never once looking my way.

As Betty and I cleared the dessert dishes and coffee cups, leaving Al and Frank to make their way to the living room, she grabbed my forearm and turned me to face her. "Madeline, what are you doing with this idiot?" she whispered. "I just don't understand how you can love someone so stuck on himself. He doesn't care at all about your feelings. How he could have talked about his marriages with such bragging enthusiasm is beyond me, especially with you sitting right there. I was embarrassed for you. You need to rethink where you are going with your relationship. There are a lot better men out there. Had he been in my house and not Frank's I would have told him off and thrown him out."

I couldn't look at her. Explaining what I felt in my heart was difficult, so I stayed silent. But I knew she was right.

Chapter Twelve

WE WOKE EARLY THE NEXT DAY. After a silent breakfast over coffee and fruit, I suggested to Al that we head back up to Little River, which was holding its annual Blue Crab Festival. I didn't want to miss it, and felt optimistic that maybe Al would appreciate this particular southern tradition. Held since 1981, the Blue Crab Festival has grown to be a world-famous event, and with nearly fifty thousand participants, one of the largest festivals of its kind in the southeastern United States.

By the time we arrived, cars were lined up all along the streets and down to the waterfront. Food kiosks by the dozens lined the Strand, as did vendors selling their arts and crafts. Of course, the blue crabs are the highlight of the celebration. Just thinking of the wonderful taste almost made my mouth water. Peals of happy laughter as friends greeted friends were all around me, but I could not fully appreciate the joyous atmosphere. I was still depressed from the night before.

Wallowing in my self-pity, I continued walking along the waterfront. Al walked beside me silently. An outdoor concert was in progress, and we stopped briefly to listen to the music. Some people sat on chairs in the shade of the live oak trees and listened, while others danced. beach music—the music of my high school and college days—blared from the speakers. I smiled wistfully at the memories. I ran into several people I knew, and hearing them welcome me back was music to my ears.

We stopped at a couple of arts and crafts booths, where Al introduced himself as a fellow artist, chatting amicably with a few of the vendors. Al acted as if nothing was wrong, and I tried to put on a happy face as well.

After about an hour, Al suggested we stop at a local café that faced the water. I sipped on a cup of hot tea while he drank a beer. There we sat, face-to-face, not saying a word to each other. Instead, we watched and ignored the elephant in the room—whose manure pile was growing by the hour. I had no idea how to escape it.

As usual, Al was keeping his eyes peeled for pretty young women. I've always known he was a girl watcher, and for the most part I've accepted it as part of his nature. Plus, there was nothing I could do about it and I didn't really find it all that threatening. Lots of men were that way. But now I found it not just threatening but maddening. I felt like there should be steam coming out of my ears, I was so close to boiling over with anger.

Of course, later that day over an early dinner, my mood once again changed. Al was back to his old charming self, chatting happily about the festival and all that we'd seen and eaten. I wasn't ignoring the fact that he'd been an ass for most of the trip, but I wanted to enjoy what was left of it without any further upset.

But in the middle of a lively conversation about one of the local artists whose work we both admired, Al's phone rang. There went my good mood.

"Yes, yes, I'm fine. I'd love to talk, but I'm driving and traffic is pretty heavy. I need to concentrate on what I'm doing. What?" A pause as the voice at the other end said something that made him smile. "Of course I'll be careful. I'll call you back soon."

Exasperated, I said, "Al, you're so full of you-know-what your eyes are even more brown than usual. You need more than a shovel to muck it out. How do you have the nerve to keep lying to people? You most certainly are not driving, except that you are nearly driving me crazy. Does that count? If this woman knew what I have learned, she would never call you again. You said that Carol only called you in the morning before classes. This is the afternoon. Another bald-faced lie on your part."

We were in public, so there was only so much I could say without actually yelling at him. Instead, I got up and walked out the door, leaving my meal unfinished. I walked down to the water, leaving Al to pay the check.

I kept checking on the front door of the restaurant to see if Al would follow me. After about fifteen minutes, I saw him walk out the door and stop at the edge of the sidewalk. He was talking on the phone. I could tell he was laughing, almost giggling. Then he saw me, held up a hand, and started walking my way. By the time he got to where I was, he had hung up.

"Al, I swear. If I get my hands on your phone I'm going to throw it in the ocean."

He merely looked indifferent, but said, "Keep your hands off my phone."

I couldn't believe it. "You win the prize for being a first-class jackass. If you don't watch out, your Pinocchio nose will grow long enough to tie a knot in it." I told him as I quickly walked away toward the pickup. He had to rush to keep up with me.

"I'm going back to the condo. You can go with me or you can stay here and take a taxi back."

Al shrugged, but kept following me to the Ranger.

Before we began living together, like Al I was lonely and thought that having a companion would be the ideal way to live out the rest of my life. I now realize that being lonely was much better than being with Al. If I could turn back the clock, knowing what I know now, I would have remained single. Maybe even converted to Catholicism and joined an order. Nuns can be nurses, too. Or I might have put more time and energy into my photography and become famous. A whole new world would have awaited me if only I could have seen the future. Too late now; the deed was done. I would have to find a way to extricate myself from this relationship and find some true happiness before it was too late.

As the day drew to a close we decided to walk along the beach before going in for the night. We parked in the drive and walked to the ocean. The air was cooler now and my lightweight jacket felt good. The beach had very few people and the tide was coming in. As we strolled along we had to dodge the water as it rolled higher on the shore. Seagulls and pelicans were scavenging for their last meal of the day. Sand pipers with their long spindly legs rushed into the receding tide in search of food. Soon they would find their perch for the night. We didn't talk at all; it didn't seem necessary. The sea sounds were soothing. I enjoyed this peaceful way to end a troubled day.

We planned to spend the following afternoon at Barefoot Landing, a shopping center and tourist destination located off the Intracoastal Waterway in North Myrtle Beach, and then meet Joan for dinner afterward. When I was growing up, the place was called Barefoot Traders. Now it was filled with upscale boutiques and restaurants. Al was always saying that he needed his space. Now I needed mine from him. A change of plans would be good for both our attitudes. I called Joan and asked her to meet me in front of Johnny Rockets for dinner. I then apprised Al of my change of plans. Surprisingly he was not disappointed.

I left him at the townhouse to swim in the pool or ocean, read, or whatever he chose. In other words, I was giving him his space. After all of our togetherness, my time alone would be more like freedom at this point in our vacation.

Arriving at the shopping center early, I browsed shops. The bookstore, Wills, had their bestsellers on display, and I decided to purchase a couple of paperbacks to read on the way back to New Haven. During my trek through the aisles I encountered a handsome man holding hands with a vivacious young woman. Her hair, clothing, and jewelry were perfect. She could have been a model. I think the devil got after me because I thought of Al and how much he would have enjoyed ogling this woman. If I told him what he had missed, it would eat his heart out. But my real interest lay in the man. He was younger than Al. He was good looking, trim, clean shaven, and meticulously dressed—definitely a 10. Remembering Al's long curly hair, shaggy beard, and disheveled clothing, he was a 4 at best, with his beach-bum looks.

By articulating the differences between Al and the dapper man, I suddenly realized that I could do much better myself. In fact, I found myself blushing thinking about whether he was as chivalrous in private as he was in public. I also thought that the physically fit stranger would probably look great in a Speedo suit and would probably fill it up quite nicely. Those thoughts made my face red, my toes curl, and my body heat up. Dead I was not! I don't know about stud muffin, but I felt he would make a great and caring lover. Fantasies were unusual for me. Obviously I needed the attention. Of course I kept that one to myself. Thankfully, it was time to meet Joan.

I paid for my book and headed to Johnny Rockets; Joan was waiting with a big smile. My, but I was glad to see my old roomie again. Her smile lifted my spirits. We had a lot of catching up to do. She was a grandmother now and was proud of it. We shared photos and chatted happily about how much she enjoyed the little one. Her cheerfulness greatly improved my dour disposition.

The restaurant had a dance floor, and several pretty young girls were trying out some Shag steps to the beach music that thumped in the background. Joan and I looked at each other and smiled as we read each other's thoughts.

"Joan, do you remember how we loved to dance?" I asked. "We could have showed those girls a thing or two. Remember how our house mother thought Shag dancing was immoral? She was very strict on us nursing students."

The girls must have thought that we looked like their grandparents. They could have been our granddaughters.

After covering several more topics, eventually the evening came to an end, and Joan and I said sad good-byes, with tight hugs and promises to visit soon.

I drove back to the beach house and parked in Julie's assigned space. Al was sitting in a recliner napping. He was startled when I entered the room. We gave each other highlights of our afternoon.

"Al," I said. "I think I will continue my peaceful day with a beach walk before going to bed."

The wind had picked up, agitating the water and causing whitecaps that looked like whipped egg whites in the impending dusk. I had planned to walk without Al, but I heard him say, "Wait up, Maddie, I want to walk, too."

I whipped around and confronted him. "No, Albert, you may not walk with me. Go for your own walk, but in a different direction, please. I want to be alone for a little while. We still need a break from each other. I will see you at the house." And with that I turned and started walking down the beach. I did not look back to see where Al was going. I didn't care.

Chapter Thirteen

For the final day of our visit, I'd planned to take Al to Brookgreen Gardens, an outdoor nature preserve and sculpture park that I knew would be appealing to both of us. After a cup of coffee, we dressed and were on our way. Midway to Pawley's Island we stopped for gas and then for a full breakfast at a local pancake house, one of many that dotted the Strand. At over nine thousand acres, it would be impossible to explore all of Brookgreen in a day, but we wanted to get in as much as possible, so a good breakfast was a must.

Back on the road again, I was surprised at the development that had occurred in the area since I had last been there. The old Myrtle Beach Air Force Base was now a large shopping center and housing development. With the building boom came traffic and more traffic. Most people would call this progress, but I wouldn't be one of them.

At least Brookgreen Gardens preserved a bit of old South Carolina. Located on four former rice plantations, the extensive gardens are home to numerous native wildlife, over fourteen hundred sculptures by 350 artists, and special exhibitions and workshops. The plantation homes and slaves' quarters are no longer standing, but graves remain in a cemetery.

A former South Carolina governor by the name of James Alston had owned one of the plantations, Oak Plantation. Alston was married to

Theodosia Burr, the only daughter of Aaron Burr, who was Thomas Jefferson's vice president. Theodosia, who grew up in New York City, did not take to the Low Country climate. To assuage her grief when the couple's only son died at an early age of an unknown illness, Theodosia decided to go to New York to visit her father. She sailed from Merrill's Inlet but never arrived in New York. The ship was presumed lost at sea. A memorial grave for Theodosia is on the grounds. The cemetery also contains the graves of her husband and child. It is said that you can see her ghost in the gardens as she keeps searching for her father.

As I was telling some of this to Al, he interrupted and asked if I'd ever seen her ghost.

"No, and I do not know of anyone who has. I doubt she haunts as far north as Little River. Do you believe in ghosts?"

Al shrugged and said, "I don't know. I have never seen one. If I did, it would probably scare the crap out of me."

I did laugh at his comment. I felt the same way.

"I am sure you remember from your history lessons that Aaron Burr killed Alexander Hamilton in a duel," I continued. "Hamilton was the first secretary of the treasury. His picture is on the ten-dollar bill. Anyway, people were angry over the senseless duel and Burr became an outcast. Theodosia worried about her father, who I'm sure is another reason for her hasty trip back home."

Soon enough we were at the gardens. Any additional history would have to wait.

"Al, why don't you look at the sculpture, and I will explore the gardens and gift shop?" I suggested.

He agreed, and we made plans to meet at the parking lot in the afternoon.

I left Al contemplating a magnificent sculpture of wild horses rearing up at each other, and I started off on one of the garden trails. Immediately I was struck by the beauty of the gardens, professionally manicured and impressive in their magnitude. Flowers were blooming at every turn. I snapped photo after photo. I knew immediately that I would set some to canvas, even though I would never be able to capture their exact beauty. Time passed quickly. When I returned to our vehicle, Al was waiting for me with a smile on his face.

"That was the best thing we have done on this vacation," he said as we made our way back to the condo. "I'm glad we came. I didn't get to study each piece as I would have liked. We simply did not have enough time. Someday I would like to return, though."

I did not ruin the moment by reminding him that he had been unhappy most of the trip—and that I had been as well.

Back at the house, we showered, dressed, packed, and closed up the townhouse. We walked to Hoskins Restaurant, a local favorite on Main Street, for a quick early-evening meal before heading back to Wilmington. I did not want to put a damper on our day but felt that Al and I needed to address some of our problems before we returned to Julie's.

"With the exception of the gardens, none of what I'd planned for this vacation made you happy. I'm sorry about that, but you knew from the beginning that I was going to my homecoming, and you also knew about the crab festival. Al, I was embarrassed that you were rude to James at the picnic. You are so arrogant that you didn't believe that a southerner could speak fluent German."

Al just raised his eyebrow and shrugged. Obviously he had forgotten about his comment and the dressing down he got. I let that issue go.

"But there is still the matter of the phone calls. We'll have to address your so-called friendship with Carol when we get back home, or I honestly don't think I can continue to live with you."

Al replied, "Look, I *have* had a good time. I don't know why you haven't. You shouldn't let the phone calls bother you. Getting back home will be good, though. Maybe you are getting too old to travel."

"Speak for yourself, Al," I stated angrily. "You're a lot older than I am." My words meant nothing to him. He didn't think he was doing anything wrong, and nothing I could say would make him understand how I was feeling. We spent the rest of the trip back to Julie's in silence.

After arriving, we sat around her kitchen table and ate the dessert she had prepared. We chatted about our trip and our activities. Al seemed to be in a good mood, but it took everything I had to put on a happy face for Julie. She suggested a game of dominos, my favorite game, but I was too weary and bid everyone goodnight. Al followed me up.

This time he kept the windows shut, even though the temperatures were much cooler since the storms had passed and mosquitoes would not be a problem. I didn't share that little fact with him, though.

I did not sleep well at all. Al and his women were foremost on my mind, and I could not turn off my thoughts. Restless, I got up to wander the house. Thankfully, I didn't wake Julie. A few months later when I finally shared with her all that had occurred, she applauded my acting abilities. She hadn't picked up on a thing.

After a quick breakfast the next morning, we packed our belongings for the last time and my dear friend drove us to the airport. She and I hugged each other tightly as we said our good-byes, tears in our eyes. I didn't know when I would see her again, but we would certainly talk on the phone.

And while the trip had not been the happy sojourn I had hoped it would be, I had finally learned the truth about Al. It was painful, but at least his behavior was now out in the open. He also knew how I felt. The elephant was still there, but it was nowhere near as large as it had been.

Chapter Fourteen

W E HARDLY SPOKE to each other on the trip back to New Haven. I for one was talked out, and we both were tired. During the flight and train ride, Al's bathroom trips were once again a frequent necessity, adding to my anger.

Perhaps my outlook would be more positive once we were back on familiar ground. In fact, I thought, maybe we should both live in New Haven full-time and keep Twin Oaks only for weekends and summer. The New Haven house was certainly large enough for both of us: a roomy bungalow with a study that Al used as an office, a separate studio for his work, and a walkout basement that I used as my studio when I stayed there. We also enjoy separate bedrooms and baths. Truthfully, this house could have used updating as well, but I wasn't about to even suggest it. One restoration project was enough. The grounds were smaller than a city lot, but Al did employ a service to ensure that the landscaping, gardens, and lawn were well taken care of. And I really liked New Haven. Settled in 1638 by the English Puritans, it is today Connecticut's second-largest city. It's also historically interesting, with many buildings and homes on the National Register of Historic Places. The old city recently celebrated its 375th birthday. And, of course, Yale University is one of the most beautiful college campuses in the world.

As we approached our street, Al became visibly anxious. As soon as the car stopped, his phone rang again and he raced inside to talk. I thought he would break the door down getting it opened. I heard him say in a slightly surprised voice, "Oh, hi there, Ginger. How are you?"

Ginger? Who was *Ginger*?

You can bet I was out of the car and in the house in a flash. As soon as Al saw me, he got off the phone.

"What's going on now, Al?"

Then he said to me nervously, not making eye contact. "Nothing you need to be concerned about. But I do need to get to the office immediately." Then as an afterthought, almost stuttering, "And we need a few things, right? Milk, eggs, bread? Something to eat for supper until you can get to the grocery store? I'll pick those up, too."

"Al, it's late. I'll pull something out of the freezer, and I'm sure whatever is going on at work can wait until tomorrow or be handled over the phone. We can go out for breakfast and go to the grocery store afterward."

"That won't work," Al said. "I need to get it tonight."

Without another word he was out the door and in the car.

Stunned, it was all I could do to sit down at the kitchen table and keep from breaking down. First Carol and now this *Ginger* person? When had I stopped being enough? Al was acting as if I wasn't even part of this relationship anymore. He had always been arrogant, but he'd also been sweet and caring. When had that all begun to change? Certainly my affections never waned. From the moment I met him I was attracted to him, to his intelligence and wit as much as his good looks. Although older than I, he had tremendous energy and was a lot of fun to be with. As I got to know him I began to appreciate just how talented he was artistically, too—a sculptor and painter of unusual and beautiful work. But that Albert had disappeared. I had just spent our vacation with a man whom I no longer knew.

About an hour later, he returned—without the milk, eggs, and bread, no less.

"Everything okay?" I asked carefully as we began to unpack.

"Yes, yes," he said, distractedly. "Listen, Maddie, given everything that happened while we were on vacation, I think you could use some time to yourself, a week or so, to work a few things out. Why don't you stay here while I go back to Oak Ridge?"

My heart sank. Al didn't care one bit about how I was feeling or if I needed time alone.

"I don't need time alone to think, Al. What I need is time with you, to *talk*."

Al sighed. "Yes, but I could really use some space."

"Why do you need your space now, Al?" I asked, exasperated. "We just got back from vacation. Are you not tired from traveling? This house is large. You can have your space here. I won't bother you. We can talk at a later date. Or are you tired of me? Go read, paint, watch TV, or whatever you do in your man cave. I don't care."

Then I paused. "Or is it that you need to see Ginger?"

Al's face turned beet red.

"Or is it Carol?" I continued. "I get confused, you seem to have so many women in your life. Tell me, does all this playing around make you feel more powerful? More sexy? Younger?"

Al started pacing. "Madeline, I know you care for me and I care for you, too. But lately our relationship has been less than passionate. Ginger and Carol are old flames, and I have to be honest with you. I want to see if those old flames still flicker, if the passion and excitement are still there."

"Is that what this is about, Al? *Sex*? I know you're looking for something different than I have given you, but you are also going through normal hormonal changes due to aging. Do you need a Ginger or Carol to "fix" every so often to feel like you are a man? Have you maybe thought that is the reason for your feeling of inadequacy, what you perceive to be your waning ability in the bedroom?"

I tried to tell him that a low libido was not unusual in an aging man and that other women could help only so much. "Al, your problems will continue. You could sleep with all the women in this town, and it wouldn't help. Women cannot medically treat you. Why don't you listen to your doctor?"

"Hormones are not my problem," he almost shouted angrily. "You don't know what on earth you are talking about. The doctors don't know what they're talking about either. You all just don't understand. Don't talk to me about a waning libido. I don't want to hear it. That is neither my problem nor yours."

I had tried before this to discuss his dilemma and treatment, but he was in denial about his problems. Sexual dysfunction was an "old man's" problem, and he wasn't old. Despite what his doctor told him, despite all that he read on the subject, Al insisted that these women would "cure" him. But I knew better. Carol would be replaced by Ginger, who would be replaced by. . . . I was heartsick thinking about it. Over time I knew the numbers of women would increase. He was right; this wasn't my problem, and there wasn't a thing I could do about it. I had a serious decision to make about my now-shattered relationship.

"Al, are you forgetting our pact? Remember, when I moved in with you, you made a promise, similar to a wedding vow, that you would not see women outside our relationship as you had all those years ago? Since when did you think being faithful was optional?"

But Al did not respond. Instead, he got in his car and drove to the Berkshires.

Though weary, I took time to call Julie to let her know that we had arrived home safely. I thanked her for her hospitality. She asked about Al, and I told her he had gone to New York and I was staying in New Haven. I did not share my problems at that time. I was too embarrassed to share what had just happened. I guess I was still in denial, still unbelieving that he had actually told me he was leaving for the Berkshires to reignite an old flame. *Careful, Al,* I thought bitterly. *Or you just might get burned.*

Shortly after talking to Julie, I got busy laundering my dirty clothes. I left Al's right where he had left them. Ginger was obviously more important than his laundry. Ordinarily I would have washed his along with mine. I was aggravated. He said they could wait, so I left them right in the kitchen. I did push them out of my path, but that was as far as I got. My petty thought was that I didn't want to mix his tainted clothes with mine.

Luckily, I still had a week off before I had to go back to the hospital—which was good, because I was a wreck. All kinds of scenarios were playing through my head, so a few days after Al left for Twin Oaks Manor I headed in that direction myself. After all, it was still my home, too, and I wanted to check on my belongings and water my plants. I had no idea who had been in and out of our home or what sort of mess I would find once there, but I had to go. I knew I would eventually have to leave Twin Oaks, and I had a lot to sort out. I would not tolerate his infidelity if it continued.

Various women visiting and not just calling had quickly become a new concern. Al and I needed to have another serious conversation about the direction his life was taking and if we still wanted to share his home. I don't think he listened to any of my tirades while on vacation. My life needed direction, too. Big decisions were looming. That seemed all I could think about. I didn't know if I wanted to continue trying to make the relationship work. Time would help me make that decision.

I didn't call to let Al know of my plans; I just packed my car and drove. As I traveled, the late spring scenery unfolding along the roadside and the distant rolling hills was a soothing distraction. Fresh shoots were emerging on the deciduous trees, and the evergreens looked brighter than usual as well. Grove after grove of apple trees were bursting with tiny white flowers. The fall's apple production would no doubt be abundant. The temperature was still cool but not unpleasant. Spring was definitely in the air.

I pulled up in the driveway about three o'clock, prepared for a fight. Instead, I found a smiling Al waving at me from the porch, where he'd been sitting with a book. He greeted me European-style, with a kiss on both cheeks, and took my luggage from the trunk and into the house.

Greeting me he said, "Hi Madeline. Welcome home. I have missed you. This old house seems empty without you in it." Since he seemed happy to see me and was acting like my old Al, I was stunned. What happened to his rendezvous with Ginger? I did not bring up Ginger's phone call, her visit, or our commitment pledges, nor did he. Hearing Al's gladness at seeing me, it seemed premature to give up on our relationship. I have to admit, I felt heartened. I am not one to throw in the towel at the first sign of trouble. I decided to stay, at least for the time being. I continued to put up with him because I loved him. That must be the reason I was there.

Later that day, over a cup of tea on the porch, I asked Al point-blank what happened to Ginger.

"She didn't show," he said, shrugging as if it were no big deal. Due to a combination of overexcitement and cell phone static, Al had misheard Ginger's "I'll be there one day soon," as "I'll be there tomorrow at noon," Turns out that Ginger also had a significant other and was having second thoughts on cheating on *him*.

I can just see Al now, racing around to ready the house, stocking the refrigerator, purchasing candy and flowers—all those things he used to do for me when I visited him in New Haven. I knew his MO well. It was all I could do not to laugh.

But what did that mean? Was Al willing to dismiss Carol and Ginger from his life for good and get back on track with me? I couldn't quite bring myself to ask the question, but he *was* being very sweet and attentive—even if he did present me with the flowers and candy that I knew had been intended for Ginger.

I threw the flowers out and put the candy in Al's room. I would give him the benefit of the doubt, but not fully buy into his program.

That evening before bed, Al asked me, "Madeline, where are my clean clothes?"

"Right where you left them, on the kitchen floor," I answered.

He actually pouted. "But you usually launder my clothes for me, and I thought you'd have done that and brought them with you."

"I tried to get you to put them in the laundry room, but you were in too big of a hurry to get to Ginger. You said they could wait."

"But I'm out of underwear," he said, sounding like a little boy.

"Well, then, it sounds to me like you need to go shopping. Oh, and when you go back to New Haven, wash them yourself."

Al looked at me sharply but didn't say a word.

After a while, we settled back into our usual routine. Al was sweet, there were no more phone calls, and we were content. Our sex life, however, was nil. I no longer wanted that from him, and his appetite had definitely waned.

One day, he started talking to me about Ginger again.

"I think that Ginger's boyfriend has been supporting her since her divorce. I think she's looking for a sugar daddy."

"If that's her intention, she'll be sorely disappointed. You need to tell her that you won't be anyone's sugar daddy. A weekend in the sack is all you are looking for, and she should know that. Don't lead that woman on."

Weeks later, however, I learned, for a fact, that Al had not pushed the other women out of his life. He was only pretending to be happy with me. Looking back I realized I had been walking on eggshells, waiting for something to happen. Perhaps I was in denial about Al's inappropriate behavior. Though wary, I tried hard to carry on as if nothing had happened. I wanted and needed for things to be as they had been before our vacation. Just thinking about the end of our relationship crushed me. I don't know why or how, but I knew I still loved this man. Sometimes it is hard for the heart to accept what the brain knows.

A loving and stable home life has always been important to me. I had grown up in that kind of household, and I aspired to duplicate it in my own life. I loved Twin Oaks Manor and was proud of the effort I put into its restoration. I considered it my home as much as Al's, and I enjoyed playing hostess over the years to a small circle of close friends who enjoyed being there and in our company. The estate was once again a showplace.

As per our original plan, the only thing left to do was turn the lower-level living room into an art gallery. I had looked forward to completing the project this fall, but since our relationship was now in shambles, my enthusiasm had waned. I no longer desired to work myself to the bone to increase the value of *his* house. What, so he could strut his stuff while I painted the walls?

Chapter Fifteen

Life continued on in a kind of limbo for several months. We were living together; we were cordial; we were, by all outward appearances, the same old Maddie and Al—except Al refused to talk about our future, and I was always on edge, waiting for the other shoe to drop.

I had to leave, so I accepted a weeklong assignment in Danbury. When I got home, I immediately knew Al had been up to something.

I confronted him at dinner. "When I was out of town last week, did you bring another woman to this house?"

"Yes, that was Susan," he admitted. "She is just another old friend. She has been divorced for a long time, and I thought being with her would be nice. We just talked and had dinner. The relationship is not going anywhere. I don't plan to see her again; she was not as great as I remembered. I remembered that she was younger than I am. But she looks old now."

"Al," I said, "does 'not going anywhere' mean you won't be having sex with her?"

He just stared at me.

I put down my fork. Here we go again. "So where did you want your relationship to go with her? Are you forgetting our pact? Remember, when I moved in with you, you made a promise, similar to a wedding vow, that you would not see women outside our relationship as you had all those years ago?"

"I'm sorry, Maddie, but I don't think I can continue to follow our pact. I need to find out if I am still attracted to my past lovers—if we're still as good together as we once were—or if I need to let go of the past. I keep thinking that maybe they will be the match to reignite my fire."

"Your fire? *What* fire?"

Al ignored me and continued, "You are a very caring person, and you have been very good to me, always taking care of me and making sure this house is a home."

"So, is that all I am? A housekeeper and a nursemaid?"

"No, no, you're a wonderful companion, but that's not enough for me anymore. Can't we renegotiate our pact? I still want you here with me, I still want to grow old with you, but I seem to want other women, too. We've known each other a long time. It's not unusual for couples our age to still care for each other but not want to have sex with each other. Is there any way you can understand that and find a way to be with me under these new terms?"

My temper was rising by the minute. "Well, Al, you've certainly reignited *my* fire, but not in the way you might think. I hear you saying that I no longer keep your fire burning. Well, guess what? You no longer stir my passions, either. You haven't been the only one disappointed. But I have accepted the changes because both of us are older, and passions do wane with age. How do you think this conversation makes me feel? When did you decide that I wasn't sexy or passionate enough for you—before or after I moved in?"

Al just stared at me, so I continued. "Say you do find the 'spark.' What will you do then? Will you ask this magical woman to live with you as you did me?"

"Maddie, please, it doesn't have to be this way. We can make this work."

"Work? How? What am I supposed to do? Find lovers of my own?"

Then something else occurred to me. "Al, have you honestly been faithful with me up to this point? Because if you have been having sex with these women and not wearing a con—"

"What is wrong with you, woman? I'm too old to get a woman pregnant. Besides, wearing a condom during sex is like swimming or taking a bath with your shoes on."

"Al, I cannot believe what you are saying. Have you truly lost your mind, or are you just stupid? You might not father a child, but you could get a disease for which there is no cure!"

I couldn't believe he would knowingly put me at risk for an STD. My stomach turned at the thought that I'd been sleeping not just with Al but with his other women and *their* other men. At this point, these women were not worried about pregnancy either. For that reason, many women are now as promiscuous as he. STDs are now on the rise with older women, women who have never thought they would become infected.

Al wasn't a nurse, so he didn't see what I did on a near-daily basis. Sexually transmitted diseases are rampant among the older generation as well, thanks in part to Viagra and the like. What was wrong with Al? Once again I found myself dumbfounded by the gulf between his book smarts and his common sense.

"And another thing," I said, my voice rising higher, "how soon will you cast these women aside if you can't find the spark that is so important to you? Do they know they're simply trial runs? What if they don't think *you're* any good in bed? What will you do then? Al, I hate what you're doing. You are destroying yourself, these other women, and me as well. Yet you don't seem to care. You seem happy with yourself, in fact. I no longer recognize you."

I paused to let him say something, anything, but he just sat there staring at me as if I was the one who was crazy. I made another attempt at logic. "And what about your approach to sex? Why is it so devoid of emotion? To you it seems to be a recreational pursuit. But to me, and to most women, it is an expression of love and devotion reserved for the most special person in one's life. Sex cannot mean that to you if you give it and take it from every woman you can. I have loved you deeply for a very long time, but it is apparent you have not loved me."

With that said, I left the room before Al could see the tears in my eyes. I needed to cry to release all these pent-up emotions, but no way did I want him to know he had that kind of power.

As terrible as it is to admit now, I stayed with Al because I didn't have the courage or energy to end our relationship, nor was I sure where I would go if I left. I was emotionally trapped—afraid of the future if I stayed, afraid of the future if I left. So I made the decision not to make a decision. Without signing any kind of document, I had tacitly agreed to Al's new terms, while hoping against hope that he would stop his philandering and revert back to the Al I had moved in with more than five years before.

I did try a new tactic. Al told me he had invited Carol to spend the following weekend with him at Twin Oaks, and asked if I would please stay at the New Haven house from Friday through Monday.

I suggested something else instead. "If I'm going to live with you on these new terms, then I think I should meet these women you are bringing into our lives. Invite her here as a houseguest. We can take her out to dinner and show her around the village."

"Are you crazy? Why would I want you here when she's visiting?"

"Because it's *my house, too*," I said through gritted teeth. "If you don't like it, then you go to her house. I'm coming back here."

"That won't work," he said slowly, as if talking to a child. "Her house is too small, and I want to be in my space, my house, with my things."

"Then be with all those things in New Haven," I said, mimicking his tone. "These women, these affairs, are *your* baggage. Don't make them mine."

"Look, Carol is unstable enough as it is. Don't make me have to negotiate these terms with her."

Lately, Al had taken to calling Carol "Crazy Carol," something that, in spite of my dislike for the woman, made me see red. "Al, please don't call her crazy. Mentally ill people don't deserve that kind of derision. Sadly, so many people take advantage of people with psychological problems and you are one of them. It's an illness, not a character flaw. Do you not know any better, or do you just not care? The way you talk, I'm beginning to think you're taking advantage of her, and that's wrong on so many levels. Not only that, her paranoia could become dangerous. I will warn you again about her diagnosis. She might stop taking her medicine, or her illness could progress without warning. Your plans could backfire. Her mental state is not a good thing. Remember, she and her husband divorced because of her mental problems. You should take her diagnosis very seriously."

But I doubt Al was even listening to me. The look in his eyes told me he was caught up thinking of the sexual things she would perform on him. His mouth was hanging open and he had a distant, dreamy look in his eyes. After reading his thoughts I said "Al, wipe the drool from your beard. It is nasty and disgusting to see." The more concern I showed, the more distance was created between us. I turned and walked from the room. My feelings no longer mattered; I could not help but wonder if they ever had. I feared that perhaps Al himself was developing a mental illness. His desire for other women was almost an obsession now. I did not understand him at all.

As a nurse, I've had some training working with psychiatric patients. As near as I could tell, Al's behavior was not normal. Who was this man? Was he a sex addict or a womanizer, or was he trying to recapture his youth by engaging in risky behavior? He seemed to be in abject denial about Carol's problems and about his own. At the very least he had developed an addictive behavior. He had become compulsive and had mood swings, and his personality seemed to have definitely changed. Once again I wondered when it had all begun. Had this happened gradually, or was this a recent problem? Was aging making a difference? Maybe I was so enamored by him that I did not notice it happening. I wondered what this would mean for me, what it would do to my own emotional well-being. Living like this was taking its toll, not only emotionally, but also mentally and physically. I didn't sleep well, my thinking was scattered, and I had lost five pounds due to a general lack of appetite.

The following day I left New York but did not go to New Haven. I was working part-time now and had planned to check into an extended-stay hotel in Danbury that was close to the hospital. Before leaving, however, I decided to put together a little welcome gift for Carol. In my pain, and despite her illness, I couldn't help but lash out at her as well. Even the mentally ill knew it was wrong to sleep with another person's partner. I left a "sweet dreams" note on Al's pillow and signed my name. Then, choosing my sexiest negligee and nightgown, I hung them in the guest bathroom and set some toiletries out on the counter. I also left a number of personal items in other areas around the house where Carol would likely see them. I wanted her to know I lived there too. I wanted to remind her that she was invading my territory. I didn't care if any of it set her off. If Al wanted her, he could deal with her.

After the weekend was over, Al called the New Haven house. Of course, I wasn't there. Then he tried my cell phone, leaving a number of messages in an increasingly frustrated voice. He had no idea where I had gone, nor did he remember my work schedule. He could have easily checked the calendar, but his agitation prevented him from thinking clearly.

I had worked through many issues while away. Not being around Al or at Twin Oaks had been extremely helpful. My anger was spent. I had become complacent. Nothing I could say would change Al. Getting through to him was impossible. I reconciled myself to the fact that I needed to live in his house a little longer to get my affairs in order before departing the scene forever. The life I had always wanted with Al was a pipedream. I once thought Al had loved me and that I was what he needed and wanted. Now I knew that I did not have him at all in the ways that mattered, nor would I ever. I would take his calls when I was ready. My backbone was finally getting stiff, and it was about time.

Two days later I decided to take Al's call.

"Why the hell haven't you answered the phone?" he barked at me. "What's going on, Maddie? Not talking to me is not like you."

"Well, this is the new me," I said. "Where I go and when I return is no longer any of your business. I considered our commitment null and void when you asked me to leave while you played around with Carol."

I continued by telling him that I decided I also needed my space, and a lot of it. Whether he liked it or not, I would come and go as I pleased. What I did was no longer any of his business. If I wanted to date other men, then I would do so. If I wanted to invite them for the weekend, he would have to leave, just as I have. Of course, I had no interest in other men. But why tell Al that?

"Oh no, Maddie. That won't work. What are you thinking, inviting other men here?"

"Al, I don't like the lifestyle you have chosen, but there isn't anything I can do about it. I can't change you, and at this point I don't even think I want to. Al I am is fed up. I will return to Twin Oaks when I'm ready. Until then, please stop calling me. And remember, two can play this game."

But instead of hanging up, Al started to assure me that he didn't plan to see Carol ever again.

I sighed. "I could care less. Do what you want."

He might have believed his words, but I didn't. Even if Carol and Ginger were truly out of the picture, surely another woman would take their place. Even if he for some reason pledged eternal faithfulness to me, everything was different now. Al should have sensed from our phone conversation that I was no longer the woman who had adored him for so long.

I eventually did go back to Twin Oaks, knowing that at some point there *would* be other women in Al's life. He was a prize-winning fornicator, and while I wanted to kick his sagging butt until it was black and blue because of it, I knew that wouldn't have stopped him. Until I was ready to move out for good, my plan was to live under the same roof as Al, but to come and go as I pleased. The only thing I asked was that he did not bring other women to the house while I was there. I told myself that I had to take my time, to consider very carefully where I would go and what I would do once I was no longer tethered to Al, the house, and our life together. It broke my heart to think of it all dissolving, and deep down I think I was hoping Al would come to his senses—that I would finally get through to him.

My biggest mistake was not sharing with anyone what was happening with me. Perhaps then someone—Julie, Joan, or my sister—would have sat me down and told me that *I* was the one being ridiculous. Al would never change, and I would always come out the loser. But, just like Al, I had my view of the world and our relationship, and I was clinging to it.

At this point, every day was a struggle. Between the emotional turmoil of worrying about Al and his affairs and the heavy patient load at work, I was exhausted. Some folks contend that adversity builds character. If that's true, then I had had about all the character-building I could take. The strain was telling. I continued to lose weight because my appetite had been almost nonexistent. Sleep was now almost nonexistent, too, and I would tear up at the slightest thing.

The next day as I drove out of town, a treat seemed in order. I swung over to a donut shop to indulge in a sweet and a cup of their special coffee. Thus fortified, I continued on to the hamlet. The tension between Al and me aggravated all the situations in my life. I dreaded seeing him and dreaded being in the house.

Everything felt tainted to me: the house, the gardens, even Al's car, on those rare occasions I had to drive it. Since I felt that our home had been defiled, I cleaned only those areas of the house that I used. One day Al noticed me cleaning the kitchen and hinted that the sauna could use a good scrub as well. I told him that I had no plans to clean the sauna, his room, or the guest room that his hussies used. I showed him where the cleaning supplies were and told him he was welcome to have at it.

I had no intention of making these conquests easy or pleasant for him or to make the house presentable for his lovers. I cleaned the house for myself, trying to wash the others away. I kept telling myself that these women were not a threat to my happiness, but deep down inside I knew that was not true. My personal foundation was crumbling, and I had no idea how to stop it or what would possibly hold me up.

There came a point where I could no longer make my life with Al work. I was grasping at straws. I had been taking one day at a time, but little by little my happiness was eroding and my life was turning into a nightmare. I needed to wake up and look at the whole picture and accept that he no longer wanted me around. I knew I had to get on with my life, but insecurity was holding me back. I decided that the house in New Haven would be my temporary sanctuary. As to the future, that was still a mystery.

During one of our rare conversations, Al confided to me that he and Carol did not go to any of the places he and I used to go, nor did they see any of our friends. They usually just stayed home and cooked.

Whether this was out of guilt or embarrassment, I don't know, but I was thankful he at least wasn't parading Carol around in public. That would have added major insult to my injury.

"Besides, I won't be seeing her again," he said. "She is hopeless and consumed with herself. I was trying to rekindle something from years ago that was special. I think this is all fantasy on my part. Madeline, you should understand that."

"I wish you'd listened to me about her mental problems, but that's neither here nor there. I don't understand you or your need for multiple women, crazy or sane, because I don't live in a fantasy world like you do. But you might have a bigger problem on your hands than your own delusions. Have you stopped to think what Carol will do if you cut it off with her? She could become dangerous. What will you do then?"

"Maddie, don't be absurd. She's not dangerous. Sure, she has problems, but they're more annoying than anything else."

"Well, at least you have one thing in common: you're both self-centered."

Al snorted. "Self-centered? I don't think so. You just don't know me and you don't understand my personality, that's all."

"Al, I've known you for going on thirty years. And now that I know you even better than before, I no longer care about you nor do I care about whatever woman you choose to have in your life. I have no hold on you. Conduct your affairs as you desire. Please, just leave me in peace. I no longer care, and I definitely don't want to hear about your affairs. I will eventually come to grips with our situation and decide what I want to do."

But Al didn't stop seeing Carol—far from it. If anything, their affair seemed to intensify. He grew obsessed with her, and she certainly knew how to add fuel to his fire. I knew that schizophrenics could become hyper-sexual, and Al once had the audacity to tell me that she was multiorgasmic. He probably strutted around like a peacock because he was man enough to satisfy her. I saw Viagra in his room, though, so apparently he wasn't the same lover of old. Without a medical enhancement, his actions would have been "Wham, bam, thank you, ma'am." Now I'm sure he thought he was king of the bedroom. What I should have said to him was, "Once a king, always a king, but once a night is enough"—although perhaps not enough for sexy Carol. *She should move in with him*, I remember thinking, bitterly. *Then they could light a fire every day as King and Queen Falk.*

But mood swings never last forever. What goes up must come down.

Chapter Sixteen

ONE DAY AL CAME BURSTING into the kitchen, startling me. I was baking bread and almost burned myself on the hot oven, looking at him instead of at what I was doing.

"I want to take a walk before it gets dark," he said, excitedly, "and then we can talk."

I wondered what he wanted to talk about. We had barely spoken in weeks. "Fine, I'll be here. Bread should be done by the time you return."

He rushed back out the door, walking stick in hand.

After only about ten minutes, he popped back into the kitchen. "Maddie, have you seen my phone? I thought it was in my pocket."

"Yes, I saw it on the kitchen counter when I was cleaning up earlier. It's right over there," I said, pointing.

I didn't say anything else, nor did I admit that I had checked his phone for calls. I knew he was nervous about that, but he didn't ask.

Without a word he took the phone, put it in his pocket, and headed back outside.

Al and I used to take those walks together, either before or after dinner, depending on our schedules, but I hadn't joined him on one since before our trip to South Carolina. So now I went alone. The exercise was energizing, and I also never tired of the ever-changing majestic views of the valley. I tried for years to capture this beauty with my camera, but my film never quite reflected the glories that I saw with my eyes.

When Al returned from his walk, I was sitting on the sofa in the family room, knitting and watching television, waiting for the bread to cool. I heard him making some noise in the kitchen. "Don't cut that bread yet!" I yelled. So often these days dinner was whatever the two of us could scrounge up. We rarely shared a table. Tonight my plans were to slather big slices of bread with butter and jam, and stay up late watching television.

A few minutes later, Al joined me in the family room, a sheaf of papers in his hand. Last week I'd written up a new proposal, in a last-ditch effort to try and salvage our relationship. Maybe this is what he wanted to talk about?

Al took a seat on one of the chairs opposite the sofa. "I have spent some time thinking about your proposal."

"Good," I said. "We need to talk about our relationship—what little there is of it. We can't go on living this way, with you seeing other women and me pretending that's okay. Our relationship is not what it once was, so we either need to end it or recommit to it."

Al set the papers down on the coffee table. "You state here that you hope I've gotten these other women out of my system and that we can go forward as a monogamous couple, but I don't think I can. I want you, too, but not the same as I did, and I don't want you the same way that I want them."

Then he paused and looked down at his hands. "You're not going to like this either, and I know it's short notice, but Ginger has agreed to come up here for the weekend. Almost angrily he said, "I want you to leave early tomorrow so I have time to prepare for her visit."

There was nothing I could say, so I stood up and walked into the kitchen. Al followed me. The bread was giving off a delicious aroma of yeast, but instead of whetting my appetite, the scent only made me sick. I wanted to pick up the loaves and throw them at Al.

"I'm not young and sexy enough for you, is that it?" I asked, dreading the answer.

Al sighed and said quietly, "To be perfectly honest, no." His purpose and use for me was over. He was shoving me aside for another not-so-important woman who had suddenly become important. I was not important, nor had I ever been nor would I ever be. I realized too late that I had never mattered in our relationship.

I let out a short, bitter, half-assed laugh. "Oh, Al, how superficial can you be? Everyone grows old, everyone watches their partner grow old. Youth, beauty, vitality, sexual prowess—all that wanes and eventually disappears. They're not what loving relationships are ultimately about. I moved in with you to share your life and, as you said, grow old together. To support and care for each other and to enjoy our retirement by experiencing the world together. Not to act like a couple of lustful teenagers. But for some reason you have come to think that sex is the most important act in a relationship. What are you afraid of, Al?"

Al set the water glass he'd just picked up down on the counter with a loud *thunk*. "Afraid? You think I'm afraid?"

Apparently I'd hit a nerve. "Yes. You're afraid of growing old. What else would explain your obsessive interest in younger women? But ask yourself: Are they interested in *you*? Why would they be?"

Despite my bravado, I was deeply hurt. The love of my life had just told me I was no longer sexy enough for him, no longer worth growing old with because apparently he now considered aging to be a character flaw.

"Maddie, when I first met you, you were young and beautiful. Vivacious. Full of life. You couldn't wait to see me. Our sex life was incredible. Remember that? But you've changed. I never see you in anything except your uniform and your cleaning and gardening clothes. You look like a housekeeper. And it's not just your exterior. You've changed inside as well, become more prim and proper. I can't imagine asking you to do the things in bed that I want to do now."

"Well, I take 'prim and proper' as a compliment. You're right: I'm not cut out for the role of a slut. And I may have been beautiful and sexy when I was young, but I was other things as well. And you didn't seem to have problems with my appearance when I was restoring your house."

Al just rolled his eyes.

"And what about you?" I continued. "You're no spring chicken, either. You're *ten years* older than I am, and you're no longer the handsome, muscular young man I met all those years ago either. You didn't age with any grace, inside *or* out. Your hair is too long, your beard too scraggly, you've grown a gut, and sometimes you walk around like everything hurts you. But now instead of accepting any of this with dignity, you've decided to throw away everything we've built together in favor of chasing skirts."

Al interrupted me with a wave of his hands. "You're wrong. Seventy is nowhere near old these days. And I don't look or act old. Old has nothing to do with age. You're as young as you feel. And I feel great."

"Oh, Al, you're delusional. Remember last fall when you met a bunch of my friends and me in that Mexican restaurant for happy hour, and you told me later you thought we looked like a bunch of old women? Well, one of my friends told me later that *you* looked too old for *me*."

When he didn't say anything, I continued. "Years ago, my friends warned me that I should think about what I was getting into with you, but I didn't listen. Not only did they think you were a womanizer, they were upset by what they perceived to be your continual putdowns. You rarely had anything nice to say to me, but I always brushed it off, putting it down to your Germanic upbringing. I realize now that my friends were right. You are borderline abusive."

"Come off your pedestal, Maddie. I'm no such thing."

Shaking my head, I said, "At least we can agree on one thing: neither of us likes each other very much. If your perverted kind of romance is what you want, then I don't want any part of it. Not many women would. You think Ginger or Carol or whoever is going to go along with what you want? Sure, they may think it's all about sex now, but just you wait. They're eventually going to want something more."

Again, my words were wasted. I don't know why I kept trying. I felt ashamed for even attempting it. There was nothing left to do but leave. My stalling and indecision had come to an end. My life with Al was over.

But instead of feeling sad and defeated, I felt flooded with intense anger. Suddenly, I became a riled dervish. With hands on my hips I shouted and said, "You really have my dander up now. How dare you say those things to me and ask me to leave again? Your words sound like it is more than just leaving. You are actually throwing me out. You can go directly to hell and stay there. You act like the devil so you should get along well!" I picked my bread loaves up off the counter, bounced one in each hand like a pitcher on the mound considering his throw, and then hurled them across the kitchen at Al. One hit him in the stomach, and the other landed on his head with a dull thud.

"What the hell is wrong with you? Are you crazy?" he shouted, rubbing his forehead.

I glared at him. "You're lucky I don't throw every bit of china and glass in this kitchen at you. In fact, you're lucky I don't tear this house apart and leave it like I found it. Maybe your next girlfriend would like to oversee *those* renovations."

Then I narrowed my eyes at him. "You have never experienced a Southern woman's hissy fit but you are now. Or should I leave the house alone and take my wrath out on your precious jewels instead? I wonder how you would look with a frilly dilly. Let's try that!" I grabbed some pinking shears from a drawer and pointed them at Al's crotch. "Snip, snip! If I castrate you, then both our problems are solved."

Very frightened and unsure of what I would really do to him, he grabbed his genitals and held them like they were the most precious things in the world. Al had never seen this side of me. I had learned by now that his family jewels were for sure his most prized possessions. His face had gone white. "You're insane," he hissed, and turned and left the room.

I let out a long, piercing shriek like a banshee and stomped my feet as if I was headed up after him. He was out the door and running up the hill by then, traveling faster than ever in trying to get away from me. I burst out laughing. What an idiot.

Unfortunately, neither destruction nor castration was a viable option for my outrage. I certainly didn't want to be saddled with a repair bill nor a summons from the police. No, my only option was to head for the house in Connecticut as soon as possible—and this time, stay away for good.

I knew what I had to do and where I was going; I had anticipated this day. One day I would return but not for the reasons he assumed. I was saddened that our state of affairs had come to this, but I had reached my limit. With 20/20 hindsight, I should have left after our trip to South Carolina, as I had thought at the time.

Chapter Seventeen

SLEEP ELUDED ME for most of the evening, but at least by the time I got up I had a plan to tackle the daunting task of packing up my things. After a quick cup of coffee and some toast, I decided to spend the morning transporting whatever I could carry in my car to a storage unit in town. When I moved in with Al, I had taken pretty much all of my furniture from my former house up to Twin Oaks. Some of it had been in my family for several generations, and some were antiques I'd picked up over the past several decades. I hated to leave these beautiful things behind. For now, though, the larger pieces of furniture, along with several rugs and lamps, would have to stay at Twin Oaks. But I could at least put them all in one spot. After two trips to the storage unit, I concentrated on moving those items from various spots throughout the house into my studio. I'd come back later with a moving company to load and transport those items, along with the items in the storage unit, back to the house in New Haven, where I intended to stay for the time being. I do not know where my energy came from, since I felt so completely drained. Irritation spurred me on. I was exhausted just thinking about the work, but I had no other option.

I have no idea what Al told his women when they asked about the home's obviously feminine touches. Did they snoop in my bedroom closet and find my skirts and dresses? Did they see the fuzzy slippers by my bed, the perfume in the bathroom? Maybe he told them it all belonged to his daughter, although some of the clothing was obviously too mature for a young woman. Or did he say these belonged to his sister or an aunt? Al had neither, but how were they to know?

The house had always been pristine, too. It was a point of pride with me. Now I could care less; it had never been my intention to keep it up so that Al could turn it into a brothel. I knew I was making a mess by moving those things I could carry safely from the upstairs to the downstairs living room. I wanted as much as possible in one place for when the movers arrived, but the fact that it made the house a shambles was an added bonus. Al would have to once again do some fancy talking. Only this time he'd have to make his excuses to Ginger instead of to me. I read somewhere once that women are angels, and even when someone breaks our wings we continue to fly— on broomsticks. That's how I felt. It was my turn to make Al's life miserable.

Ginger was due to arrive by five o'clock, but by one I still wasn't finished. Al followed me out to the car with a worried look on his face.

"I'm trying to get as many of my things in my storage unit and studio as possible," I said before he could open his mouth. "Then I'll pack my car for the trip to New Haven. That's what's been taking so much time. I'll send movers for everything that I can't take now. So don't worry; I have no desire to meet your whore. I'll be gone before she gets here."

"Don't you dare call her a whore!" Al said, angrily. "There's nothing wrong with liking sex, and I don't pay her."

I laughed. "Al, as far as I'm concerned a *prostitute* charges for sex. Whores give it away without asking anything, like love or loyalty, in return."

I noticed that the word "movers" also went over his head. I think he was surprised that I had done more than just fill a suitcase for a weekend trip to New Haven. He was also obviously nervous that I wouldn't be finished in time for him to get ready for Ginger. "Here, let me help you," he said. "We'll fill my car, too. That'll be quicker."

Hah, I thought, *he thinks we're going to take another load to the storage locker.* Little did he know I now planned to pack up my clothes, toiletries, knitting, and a few books and head up to New Haven. I thought I'd string him along for a bit.

"Okay, thanks," I said. "You can follow me then."

When both vehicles were packed, we took off down the driveway. After about five miles, I realized Al was no longer behind me. Then my cell phone rang.

"Where the hell are you?" Al asked angrily. "I thought you were going to your storage unit."

"I'm on my way to Connecticut. Where do you think I'm going? I've already been to my storage unit and don't have time to go again. You said you wanted me gone by five o'clock, so I'm complying."

"For crying out loud, I can't go upstate now. I have things I need to do before Ginger gets here in a couple hours."

"Well, since you don't have a key to my storage unit, you'll just have to take my things home with you. Ginger can help you unpack. Just, please, don't damage anything or let it get stolen."

"I don't know what I'm going to do, but I'll think of something. Moving you was not part of my plan today."

"It wasn't part of mine, either," I said, and ended the call.

I laughed at the thought of leaving Al's SUV jam-packed with my belongings and the house such a mess. If he and Ginger wanted to go out, he'd have to unpack. If they wanted to stay in, they'd have to hang out at the dining room table because I'd moved the sofa and chairs. Perfect. I was angry but also strangely elated. I was finally moving out—finally free of Al's lies and manipulations. I knew that eventually I'd have to deal with the underlying humiliation and sadness, but for now I felt relieved.

I had already let this go on too long. I'd made too many excuses for Al's behavior, and for mine. I didn't want to live that way anymore, and there was no going back. Al had changed and was beyond help. It was time to move, literally and figuratively, into my future and into happiness.

I had a lot of time to think during the long drive. I still felt insecure, but at least I was no longer panicked. The romantic stars were finally gone from my eyes. I felt empowered, but also intimidated by the work that lay ahead of me. "Take it slowly," I told myself. "Baby steps." The first was to get to New Haven. Once there, I'd at least have a roof over my head, a place from which I could take further action. I had to remember that things always work out. Now I would see how they worked out for me.

I had sorted through some of my emotional pain but knew I had a long way to go before I was completely healed. That would take years. Some scars might never disappear. I wondered why some people fall so wholeheartedly for the wrong person, as I had done. Some spend the remainder of their lives trying to understand and recover from it. I knew I would do the same.

I was exhausted when I finally got to the house in New Haven. Still, I felt the urgent need to call Julie and tell her what had happened.

"What? You mean that scoundrel threw you out of the house *you* restored?" she said. "Once bitten, I always say, but you were so convinced that this time would be different. I have to admit that I liked him, too, after my visit a couple years ago. And he seemed so content when y'all were down here in May."

"Yeah, well, that was because he was thinking about other women," I said.

"Maddie, I'm so sorry your life has come to this. I don't understand why it's taken you so long to leave the jackass. You should have left before he threw you out. You became his doormat, and that's not like you."

"I didn't want to act in haste, and I never thought of myself as a doormat. I was trying to honor our commitment. I wanted to make sure it was truly over, that there was absolutely no hope, before I hauled my ass out of there." I couldn't help but laugh at my language.

"Good grief, Maddie. Commitment doesn't mean a thing to Al, and it never will. His ass is the one that should be leaving."

"I'll tell you another thing, Julie," I said. "Al drove me out of one house that I thought I would live in for the rest of my life, but I'll be dadgummed if I'll let him run me out of another. I'll live in New Haven as long as I need to."

"Now you're talking," Julie said emphatically. "Have faith in yourself. You and Al need to let each other go. You may be good for him, but he is horrible for you."

I felt better about everything after our talk. Julie's no-nonsense encouragement was just what I needed. I could tell her things that I couldn't tell another soul, and she always put things in their proper perspective.

"It's over," I said aloud. "It's really over."

Pain twisted my heart and manifested in other areas of my body as well. I washed up, took some Ibuprofen, and got into bed, burrowing under the covers like a bear in its den. Sleep came quickly, and I slept like someone sedated. When I woke the following day, I realized that I had slept almost around the clock. Thankfully my headache was gone, and I felt like a new person. Most of my tension had been left in the Berkshires. My energy renewed, I searched the cupboards for something to eat, settling on a cup of hot tea and a peanut-butter-and-jelly sandwich. It would have to do until I could get to the grocery store. In the meantime there was work to be done. Once again I arranged my belongings in a house that wasn't mine.

The weekend following my banishment from Twin Oaks Manor, I returned for my furniture and other personal items that I was unable to take in my car during my initial exit. During my week away, Al had called several times, both on the landline and on my cell, but I never picked up. "Let him wonder," had been Julie's advice, and I took it. He'd signed off his last message with an exasperated, "I can't believe you're being this childish. Fine, just let me know when you plan to come home."

When I arrived, Al met me at the door. He looked tired but seemed glad to see me.

Ushering me inside, I noticed he had a splint on his right wrist.

When I asked what happened, he said he'd tripped and fallen during a hike in the woods. "Sprained my wrist something awful," he said, wincing. "It hurts like the devil. Maybe you can check it for me while you're here. Tell me what I need to do to help the swelling and soreness."

If he had intended to invoke my sympathy, he was sorely mistaken. Those days were long past. I would be his nurse no more.

"Bless your clumsy old heart," I said with mock sweetness. "Good luck using your left hand."

"Sheesh, Maddie, I could have been seriously injured. Is that all you have to say?"

I sighed. "Al, I really could care less about your wrist. I'm sure your doctor has given you some good advice on what to do in order for it to heal."

"Speaking of 'caring less,'" Al said, "what was the big idea, leaving this house in such a mess when you left? It was embarrassing."

I stopped walking and turned to glare at him. "Al, you *threw me out*, remember? Gave me only hours to leave. What did you expect?"

"I expected you would only pack a bag for the weekend and then come home. Like always." He sounded like a spoiled little boy.

"No, Al, I meant to leave you for good. In fact, that's why I'm here today. To finish what I started."

At that moment I heard the roar of a truck engine. The moving company had arrived. Al parted the living room curtains and turned to me with a panicked look on his face. "What's going on, Maddie?"

Alas, the poor baby thought I was returning to live with him again. How sad. Had he forgotten about all the things I had removed the week before? Jiminy Christmas, talk about denial.

"I'm finishing moving my things out, that's what I'm doing. After the truck is loaded, I'm going back to Connecticut to live. It's my home now. Do you want me to move your things to the basement, or should I arrange to have them sent here?"

"What do you mean, 'live there'? I thought you would come back here to live with me as we planned. Damn it all, Madeline, this is not how I planned things to work out. I want you here. You know how depressed and lonesome I get when you aren't here. When I need you, I want you here. I haven't been feeling well. What will happen to me if I get really ill?" He was actually whining now.

"Well, as you've said yourself, you're not old. If you get sick, you'll recover. And don't give me that 'need' bull. You might need me, but you don't want me. There's a big difference. Your happiness is your number-one priority and always has been. Now my happiness has become my top priority."

"Look, can we talk about this? We could go to the Brewery for dinner tonight and talk this out. We can make this work."

"Baloney, Al. I don't believe you. You're just trying to get back into my good graces by placating me. You think you can talk me into moving back in with you? That might have worked at one time but not any longer. You never intended to honor our commitment. Thinking back, I doubt you ever took it seriously. Your dalliances were more important than I was, and you completely ignored my unhappiness once you started fooling around."

I continued by telling him that I no longer trusted him or believed anything he had to say. Our relationship as we once knew it was over. I had tried hard to make it work, but I couldn't fix his problems. It takes two people working 100 percent at a relationship to keep it going.

"Never again will I be your doormat. You have used me for the last time. I should have left months ago, but I wanted to give you more time to come to your senses and see what was really important in our lives. But you can't have me and have other women, too. That just won't work for me. You think you understand women, but you have no idea what we want or need, nor do you understand anything about our feelings."

Twice he said we would marry. For five years I lived with him waiting for that pledge, but he never honored it. And I knew now he never intended to. As Julie once said, a man who wants to marry a woman asks her then and there, he doesn't keep putting it off until some "perfect" day and time. I had no desire to marry him now or ever. I was sorry I ever let him talk me into living with him. I was sorry that I was so emotionally blind that I could not see him for who he was.

"I thought I was special, Al. What a crock. You wanted me, but you wanted me without the official commitment. But it just doesn't work that way. I see that now."

Al started to say something, but I stopped him. I didn't want to hear anything he had to say.

"And now you dare question why I'm leaving you, when you *threw* me out so you could invite one of your hussies over for a weekend of sex? No woman in her right mind would put up with that. I'm glad I finally saw just how sick you are."

"Hold your horses, Madeline. Back up a minute. The house is mine, not yours, and we are not married."

"No, you wait a cotton-picking minute," I said, hands on my hips, my eyes narrowed to menacing slits. "I know you technically own the house, but I spent countless hours making it a home. You *invited* me to live here. You insisted I sell my home and come renovate this one, with the promise that we'd build a life together here. You certainly enjoyed the income I brought with me and the backbreaking work I did to restore this house, a house you let fall into shambles. And while I was surprised at your lack of participation, it didn't discourage me because you kept telling me I was doing it for *us*. Now you have tossed me out. In exchange for losing this house, I will finish moving into yours in New Haven, and live in it until I decide where to go from there. You'll just have to find other sleeping arrangements when you come to town to teach. I absolutely will not sleep under the same roof as you."

I had always envisioned a normal, genteel, and secure way of life for myself, which included a partner with whom I could enjoy a mutually loving and respectful relationship and who shared my love of travel and art. I thought that's what Al had wanted, too. Too late. I now knew that I would never have a normal life with Al.

"Al," I said, "I have put up with your whores, your mood swings, your compulsive behaviors, your self-serving ideas, and with you in general. I'm finished now. Our days of talking and reconciling our problems are long over. It will be better if we don't see each other again."

Then I went outside to give directions to the movers. Together we began to load up my things. Al just stood there, a frustrated look on his face. He knew better than to argue with me in front of strangers, so after a few minutes I heard him stomp off to his office and slam the door. There was nothing more to say, as far as I was concerned. I had said the words that needed to be said—words that I had planned to say when the time was right. That day must have been the right time because the words rolled off my tongue.

While going from room to room to make sure I had all my things, I discovered a lacy black negligee crumpled in a corner of Al's bedroom. But for some reason the bed in the guest bedroom had been slept in. That struck me as funny: Al and Ginger performing all kinds of sexual gymnastics, but when it came time to actually *go to bed*, they each went their separate ways. Maybe Ginger snored, or Al had started talking in his sleep. Regardless, Al had not cleaned up after her or after himself. I assume he thought I would be returning to do it. After all, he had a sprained wrist, poor thing. How could he possibly be expected to change the sheets and do laundry?

Once the movers and I had filled up the truck with all my possessions, the once-lovingly decorated house looked like an empty shell. Surely Al would be shocked once I was gone and he made a tour of the rooms. For a split second I felt bad for him, but then I willed my anger to return. This was *his* doing, not mine. I no longer cared what his plans were or if he had furniture to sit on, a pot to pee in, or a window to throw it out of. I was royally teed off. In fact, I would have left him with a parting

"Go f— yourself, Al," if I hadn't thought it would make my poor mama turn over in her grave. At least I could stick him with the bill, since I had charged everything to Al's credit card. I'd bet he'd forgotten I even had it.

Now all that was left was to head to my storage unit and load up those items. But I made one last tour. I did not want to leave anything behind.

One last tour, one last look around, and it was time to go. I didn't want to linger, to slip into sadness and nostalgia, but I did knock on Al's office door to tell him I was leaving.

To my surprise he opened it. I steeled myself against the look he gave me, one both sad and perplexed. "Maddie, please, don't do this. At least tell the movers to come back in the morning so we can talk and you can sleep on this."

Do not let him manipulate you, I said to myself. And then, out loud, I told him, "Al, I no longer love you, or even like you. You've killed my love, my respect. You want a different life; I want a new one. The two are incompatible. I have finally accepted that you needed me but did not love me. You really never saw me for who I was. You saw a maid, a gardener, a caregiver, a companion, but you never saw a whole person with feelings. You will never find another woman like me. And you certainly won't find one who will tolerate your womanizing."

With that, I walked out the door of Twin Oaks Manor.

Chapter Eighteen

I DIDN'T SHARE THE GORY DETAILS of the breakup with my friends and family. It was enough that they knew I had left Al for good. But one of our mutual friends, Phil, who taught at Yale and lived in New Haven, was well aware of Al's philandering. He called me up one day to see if I was free for a cup of coffee. He wanted to give me a thumbs-up in person and let me know he was on my side.

Over a couple of cappuccinos, he told me he had never condoned Al's behavior. "I couldn't believe how boastful he was," Phil said, shaking his head. "I told him that he was making a huge mistake, risking the best thing he'd ever had, but he wouldn't listen to me."

He went on to tell me that Al hadn't actually sprained his arm tripping over a root in the woods. Because I had removed the sofa from the living room, Al and Ginger had to rig a makeshift one. Sitting led to other things, and in their sexual acrobatics they became so entangled in the ill-fitting sheets they fell to the floor. Al landed on his arm, and Ginger landed on top of him.

"I can't believe he'd share that with you!" I said, and laughed.

Phil cracked a smile. "Yeah, well, you know Al. Talk about going down in a hurry. Of course, Ginger had to take him to the emergency room."

I could see it now: a twenty-five-mile midnight ER run that left them hungover the next morning is not the height of romance. Realizing he had to use his left hand to zip and unzip, eat, drive, and so on gave me great satisfaction.

Again, I must say that I no longer recognized the man Al had become. Men need to understand that women are usually flexible. We try to be peacemakers. Even though we might not forget, we do try to forgive. There are times, though, when we are unable to do either. I had certainly reached that point.

Still, it was a daily struggle not to let the pain of my loss become crippling. I was angry, yes, but I was also hurt and in mourning. It's a terrible thing to be rejected by someone you love and to realize that perhaps they did not love you in return. My love for Al had been deep and unfailing, and yet it was all for nothing. In many ways the loss of a relationship is not unlike the loss of a loved one. One goes through similar stages of grief.

I also knew that I was not alone. Many husbands and lovers treat their spouses as Al had treated me, sometimes worse. I wondered if they were also afraid to show their anger, to stand up for themselves, out of a fear of losing whom they thought was the only person who would love them. In my case, I didn't want to make our situation worse and cause Al to turn away even more. I thought that, if left alone, he would eventually see the light.

Getting beyond the agony was necessary for my survival, but it would not be easy. Throughout my life I have met my problems head-on, dealing with them quickly and without emotional bondage. My coping mechanisms were failing me this time. Helping my patients with problems was much easier than helping myself. I knew that suppressing my feelings would drain my energy, energy that I would need to focus and redirect my life. Yet I was basically afraid to express how I really felt. I did not want to overreact or lose control like I had when I threw things at Al.

It had helped *me* to vent at Al before I drove away from Twin Oaks Manor, but as far as I could see, it had gone right over his head. More than anything, I felt a deep need to make Al understand just how destructive his philandering had been—to realize what we both had lost. And if I didn't necessarily want to be friends with the man, I knew that I'd run into him if I was to remain in New Haven, and I wanted to do so without throwing things at him. But it was a delicate balance. I was angry and justifiably so. But I was also afraid that if I expressed that anger, Al might throw me out of this house, too. I knew I would leave eventually, but for the time being I didn't need the added pressure of looking for and purchasing a house. I needed to make realistic plans that were in my long-term best interest. I couldn't afford to do anything rash or make another mistake. I was all alone this time, so it was imperative that I put my best foot forward.

Working in Danbury had certainly helped me stay sane. When I returned to work part-time, it was like returning home—which, of course, Danbury was, since I'd lived there for over two decades before moving in with Al. When there, I rented a suite at an extended-stay motel. Oddly enough, this worked for me. I was busy while in Danbury and didn't have time to think about Al or the fact that so much of my life was in limbo. When I did feel depressed, I would garden, paint, draw, or write a poem expressing my feelings. I could see glimpses of the old Madeline peeking through the darkness.

Three months had gone by since I had moved out, and Al had tried to call at least once a week during that time. I never picked up, and I erased his voice messages without listening to them. I didn't fool myself into thinking he was worried about me. Most likely there was something he wanted. I had no idea where he stayed when he was in New Haven, and I didn't care. He never came by the house, which I found interesting. There were things there he likely needed, but I never saw him and he didn't use his key to let himself in when I wasn't there. I'm sure he didn't want to face me, the coward. Phone calls were much safer.

One day I finally answered his call.

Typical for Al, he launched right in without preamble. Didn't say hello, didn't ask how I was doing, didn't ask why I never returned his calls. "Maddie, how would you like to go to New York City with me?"

"Seriously, Al?" I asked, feeling the old anger beginning to rise.

"I've been doing some thinking," he stuttered, as if trying to find the right words. "It wasn't until you moved out that I realized how unhappy you were. You always came back, and I thought you would again. I have to go to New York, and I really don't want to go alone. I know you love the city and thought you'd appreciate a break. And we could, you know, *talk*."

"What's going on, Al? Did you fall off the furniture again and hit your head? Because you sound a little crazy."

Silence. He didn't know I knew about the sofa, and I laughed inwardly at the dig.

"Nothing is wrong with me," he finally said.

"Actually, Al, I had planned to go into the city sometime soon because a good friend is having a showing at one of the galleries. But I'm not about to go with you. Why don't you call one of your ladies of the evening instead?"

"I don't have many friends who are interested in looking at art," he said. "But I know you are. We can go together but not necessarily go everywhere together. Do our own thing, then meet up for dinner before taking the train back."

I didn't know if I was ready to see Al yet. We had only been apart a few months, and I was still combating feelings of anger and shame. Then again, maybe it would help me heal, spending time with him with no expectations beyond discussing a mutual interest.

"Okay, Al, let me think about it. I'll call you in a day or so."

I slept on it. In the morning I decided that I would put aside my feelings and accompany Al on a day excursion into the city. It was a test of sorts for myself: Could I be around him without falling back into old patterns of behavior and without old feelings rising to the surface, or could I remain neutral?

The trip was a marathon, with visits to the Metropolitan, the Frick, and several art galleries, including the one hosting my friend's show. I took the afternoon to do some shopping, while Al popped in to several more galleries. We would meet up separately for dinner, at Paesanos in Little Italy, an Italian restaurant we both knew well. When the time came for me to hail a cab, I realized how exhausted I was. I had made similar treks many times in the past, but I didn't remember feeling quite as tired as this. Darn it, age was rearing its ugly head again.

In spite of the flurry of activity, Al and I had been tense and uncomfortable with each other. We didn't quite know how to interact with each other, so we compensated with silence or extreme politeness. I realized several times that I was keeping my lips pursed to prevent me from going on another tirade. But anger was good. It was better than nostalgia and sadness.

I thought maybe we would be more relaxed at dinner. Al was already seated by the time I arrived. He'd chosen the garden room, which was peaceful and just what both of us needed. We ate mostly in silence, but this time it was more the silence of relaxation and enjoyment. The meal was excellent as always, and I even indulged in one of their cannolis, the perfect ending to a perfect meal. We capped the evening off with coffee for Al, a cup of hot tea for me. The restaurant had filled up in the meantime, and the other diners were having a grand time. It had been a long time since I had been in the company of such happy people. I missed that. It was still early when we finished eating. We went outside and flagged down a cab to take us to the train station.

Al was in obvious pain from all the walking we'd done that day, but he didn't complain. He seemed addled, too, which was puzzling. He knew the city better than I did, since he grew up there. Perhaps he was simply overly tired. We had covered a lot of territory while walking.

Returning home, both of us were lost in our thoughts. The train's motion almost lulled us to sleep. Our age was definitely showing. At one point, Al made an attempt at conversation. He told me that he'd made plans to go skiing with his daughter and stepdaughter the following weekend. "I don't see them enough," he said, with a bit of sadness in his voice.

When I expressed mild surprise, given the way he'd been hobbling earlier, he dismissed my concerns with a grimace. "There you go again, Maddie, always thinking I'm an old man."

And there he went again, always countering my concern with denial. Still, I was glad I'd gone with him. The trip confirmed that I still enjoyed seeing great art, but also made me realize something much more important: I no longer enjoyed Al's presence. I had agreed to join him because I needed to prove to myself that my feelings for him had changed. I didn't want to second-guess my decision. Happily, I realized that my trust and love in him were long gone, and I was actually enjoying living by myself again. I don't know what I had been dreading.

Then Al started speaking again. As I had suspected all along, he'd only asked me on the trip in order to get something in return. "Since you moved out, I have given a lot of thought to our relationship," he began. "I finally realized that you meant what you said and that our living arrangement was over. I must confess that I have missed your handling all the details of our life."

I wanted to say, "I told you so," but I kept my mouth shut.

And I noticed that he did not say that he had missed *me*, only what I *did*—which was to handle all the bills, do all the grocery shopping, cook all the meals, clean the house, and keep the garden in order. Who was doing that for him now? I wondered. Certainly he wasn't doing anything himself.

"So I'd like to propose that you take over where you left off. Except I would pay you."

Before I could say anything, he went on to explain that he would like me to oversee Twin Oaks Manor while he was away, which included starting the process of listing the house on the National Register and completing the conversion of part of the downstairs into an art gallery.

I was speechless.

"What do you say?" Al prodded.

I just shook my head and laughed. "No, Al."

"Don't decide now. Take the rest of the weekend to think about it and get back to me."

Once back in the safety of my home and away from Al's influence, I spent about 2.5 seconds considering it. Even that small amount of time made me ashamed of myself.

There was no way Al's proposition would work for me. I did not want to be caught in his web again. That spider had spun me tightly one too many times.

The next morning I called him with my decision. "The answer is no, Al. How would I feel if one of your women came to visit when I happened to be there? I know you would want me to expand my role and return to being housekeeper, nurse, or anything else that you needed. Working with or for you is a bad idea. I would be the loser again. I distrust you completely, and I profoundly doubt that you can ever regain my trust. I learned my lesson the hard way. I will never allow you to dupe me again."

Al was disappointed. He didn't understand why I would refuse to do something like this. He thought I would be delighted to be back at Twin Oaks again. "No one knows that house and grounds like you do, Maddie," he said. But if he thought he was appealing to my vanity, he was wrong.

We ended the conversation as amicably as possible. I knew that establishing an art gallery would have been fun, but my enthusiasm for the project—in fact, my enthusiasm for anything connected to Albert Falk—had died. I was pleased with myself that I could say no and really mean it.

Chapter Nineteen

WHILE I WAS MOVING MY THINGS out of Twin Oaks Manor, I accidently packed Al's journal. He must have inadvertently filed it away on the bookshelf in the living room, and in my haste I took it with me, thinking it was part of my section of books.

I discovered it one rainy Saturday afternoon when I was rummaging around in some boxes, looking for a novel that I'd been reading before I left. As soon as I opened it, I realized what it was. I shut it quickly, as if it were on fire, and set it down on the coffee table. I had no idea Al kept journals—introspective was one of the last words I'd use to describe him—and I wasn't sure if I wanted to know what was inside.

I put my decision off by making a cup of tea and going through the rest of the box. Every now and then I'd glance at the journal, hoping that maybe it had disappeared and I wouldn't have to deal with it. Finally, I let my curiosity get the better of me. With a mixture of excitement and dread, I curled up on the sofa with a second cup of tea and opened the journal to the first page.

It wasn't a journal so much as a catalogue of sexual escapades. I didn't know whether to be shocked, angry, or worried. The ego behind the pen was much larger than I'd ever suspected. Every woman he'd ever bedded was in there, along with detailed descriptions of what they looked like, what they liked in bed, how he rated their techniques, and sometimes even explicit details of what they had done together. I had never heard him use such language. Needless to say, he did not evaluate himself. Why did he feel the need to write down his affairs at all? Maybe his memory was going quicker than I thought, or maybe he wanted a testament to his prowess. I suppose I wasn't memorable enough to earn even an honorable mention, because there was nothing in there about me. Thank goodness for small favors. I needed to wash my eyes out with soap to remove the dirty words they had read,

Al's first encounter with Carol since their breakup must have been special, because he wrote at even greater length about her. Several months before I moved in with him, I discovered, he had invited Carol up to Oak Ridge Village for the weekend. He wrote about how inconvenient it was to have to pick her up at the train station because she didn't drive, but then again, he wouldn't have to worry about neighbors seeing a strange car in the driveway and a strange woman going in and out his front door. On the way to the house, they stopped for a bite to eat in a restaurant that is known for attracting a young, rock-and-roll type of crowd. Supposedly it has black crosses on the walls. The waitresses are scantily clad and have black tattoos and body piercings, and they wear heavy black eye makeup. He wrote that he chose it because he didn't want anyone he knew to see them together.

My whole reason for inviting Carol to visit was to get her back into my bed, Al wrote. *I wanted her to myself and without any chance of interference. Shortly after we arrived home, I served her a drink. We relaxed and chatted. We listened to romantic music while continuing to enjoy our wine. We spoke little, instead concentrating on kissing and touching each other. When she was ready for sex, I was more than ready and gladly complied.*

I imagine Al must have strutted like a peacock because he had satisfied Carol's sexual needs. She even called him, he wrote, her "stud muffin."

After a while, Al continued writing, she asked for more sex. Al was more than agreeable, so he led her into his bathroom for more foreplay in the old claw-foot tub. He turned on the water while Carol excused herself to dress in her French maid outfit, forgoing, Al wrote, her panties. The short skirt just covered her cheeks.

Man, that was great, so sexy. I was fully aroused and I wanted sex more quickly than I thought. Carol bent over slightly to show that she wasn't wearing underwear. I became very excited and could hardly wait. She climbed in the tub to straddle me, sloshing some water over the sides of the tub. But neither of us cared. We were both in the throes of passion. I could hardly wait for sex and became frustrated trying to unzip the front of her uniform. Finally I managed it, releasing her luscious breasts.

Al then went on to describe in painstaking detail everything they did to each other—apparently all the while completely oblivious to the fact that the tap was still running. According to Al, Carol was the first to fully realize that something was wrong. *Carol broke free from my embrace, hopped out of the tub, and let out a yell. "The tub is running over,"* she screamed. *"Water is everywhere. The bathroom and hallway are soaked."*

The tub is old and does not have a drain out the back to prevent overflow. Instead, the water from the bathroom had run down the hall, soaked the rug, and leaked between the cracks in the old wooden floor to the ceiling below. So this was the "burst pipe" Al had told me about—the mess I had cleaned up. How insulting that I had restored the damage that he and Carol had caused. I wondered if he had been laughing behind my back while the contractors replastered the walls?

Getting busy, Al and Carol picked up the rugs so that they could mop up the water with towels. What a sight that must have been, two coots running around the house naked as jaybirds, trying to soak up that amount of water with towels. They probably used every towel Al owned. Did either of them not know how to use a mop and pail? Talk about putting a damper on a romantic weekend.

Al called his insurance company the following morning. They sent a recovery crew to take care of the moisture reduction and to prevent mold, setting up huge industrial fans both upstairs and down. The crew recommended he take care of the damage right away, since repairs and cleaning would cost much more in the future, but Al decided to put it off until a later date.

Apparently the noisy fans created tension between the lovebirds. *With the fans blasting away we got into a heated argument. Carol talked endlessly in circles, with so much repetition that I could not understand a thing she said.*

According to Al, Carol knew about his other dalliances, but she demanded he see her exclusively. She even wanted to move in with him. They spent the rest of their "romantic" weekend arguing about it, leaving an exhausted Al to exclaim in his journal that he was thinking about breaking it off with her. He liked that she was sexually experimental—and he got a thrill out of knowing that some of their escapades had made it into her erotic novels—but she was proving to be too clingy.

Chapter Twenty

I HAD A SETBACK a few months later when, during a visit downstate to an art exhibition, I decided to invite Kate and Margaret, a couple of friends from Oak Ridge Village, to lunch. I told myself not to drive past Twin Oaks Manor while I was there, but eventually curiosity got the best of me. I told myself that I was strong enough by now to handle it.

I was wrong. I should not have gone. Memories of my time there— of the house and the gardens that I had restored, of the village and the friends Al and I had made—came flooding back, and I became weepy from regret and what I can only describe as homesickness. While I didn't miss Al, I did miss the Al he once was and the potential of all that we could have shared together.

I had an hour before meeting my friends for lunch, so I decided to check in on Ethel, a longtime resident about twenty years my senior with whom I'd become close. Ethel welcomed me with a warm smile and a hearty hug. Ushering me into the kitchen, where she put the kettle on to boil, she asked me where I'd been. "I've missed seeing you in the garden and out and about in the village."

"Al and I aren't together anymore," I said quietly. "We decided we needed to go our separate ways. Both of us want different things in life."

Needless to say, she was concerned. It was obvious she didn't know anything about Al's other life. In my opinion, the fewer people who knew about his women, the better. Maybe I was being self-centered, but Al's behavior was an embarrassment to me. This fine lady did not need to be embarrassed, too, so I did not go into great detail about our split. Besides, given his family history in the neighborhood, Al's reputation was important, whether he cared about it or not.

Ethel was happy to catch me up on the local goings-on. After five years, I had made the acquaintance of many people in the village. Some were even friends, but even they didn't know the whole story behind my leaving Al. My visit had cheered me up greatly. Ethel had that ability; it was one of the qualities that had quickly endeared her to me.

Finally, it was time for lunch. I'd asked Kate and Margaret to meet me at the Purple Onion, a café at which we'd spent many hours over the years indulging in girl talk and enjoying great food. Our usual table by the window was available, so we sat there. I was happy to see that not much had changed. Paintings of various onion varieties hung on white walls with purple trim, and the wait staff wore purple aprons with embroidered onions on the front. We placed our orders with Eileen, our longtime server, who gave us a hearty welcome.

"I can tell you ladies are just dying to catch up with each other," Eileen said. "I'll get your order in immediately. Enjoy yourself and don't forget to share with me if you think I would be interested in anything juicy."

Before long we were laughing and gossiping just like old times. Customers indulged us with knowing smiles. Who could resist three ladies having such an obviously good time? My girlfriends knew that I had moved out, but not much beyond that. So far I had not shared the full details with anyone but Julie. I felt secure with Kate and Margaret, though.

"Al decided that he needed more than one woman in his life," I began. "And he actually thought I'd go along with it. That I'd let him have his cake and eat it, too. No way would that work for me, so I moved to New Haven."

Kate and Margaret exchanged looks. "What a rat," Margaret said. "Good for you for moving out. What woman would agree to living like that?"

"He must be off his rocker," Margaret said. "A lot of us think that. You're the best thing that ever happened to him. It's rare that we ever saw him with a woman of your caliber. After Joyce, every woman he brought around the village just looked tawdry. Joyce was a nice person and a lady as well. We've never been able to figure him out. He marries or has long-term relationships with upstanding women, but he cheats with trash. How on earth did you live with him for so long?"

"Thanks for the compliments, ladies, I really appreciate your support. Al does have some good qualities, but it took me a long time to wise up to his shenanigans. He was very deceitful. Other people have told me similar things about him. Al doesn't see what others see in me. I suppose he's comfortable around me because I'm sensible and orderly. And you can bet he appreciated the fact that I did all the chores and took care of all the bills. But he doesn't want that full-time. He thinks he needs more passion in his life and that only younger, more sexually free women will give that to him. His passions do not include nice, respectable women."

"Maddie, I am glad you finally moved out," Margaret continued. "Bert probably will never change, and you were wasting your life waiting for him to come to his senses. I do miss having you around, though. We've had fun solving everyone *else's* problems."

That made me laugh, but Kate remained serious. "Maddie, it really bothers me that you put up with that kind of treatment. You're one of the smartest women I know. I just can't figure it out."

I shook my head. "I've asked myself the same thing a hundred times. I suppose Al's not the only one who needs therapy. I see him more clearly now, but I still do not, nor probably ever will, understand him. He really did change from the man that I fell in love with."

Margaret and Kate began sharing more about what they knew of Al's behavior. Perhaps they had wanted to tell me these things for a long time but didn't dare because they knew how I felt about him. Now they seemed relieved to finally get a few things out in the open.

"The local gossip is that Bert has been running around for years," Kate said. "We think that's why Joyce finally divorced him." They then told me about Adele, a woman who lived in the neighborhood. Born and raised in Austria, Adele was an exotic beauty who first caught Al's eye when Joyce hired her to work as a maid at Twin Oaks. After the divorce, Al pulled out all the stops in an attempt to seduce her. Turns out it was just that: an attempt. Adele had in the meantime become very good friends with Joyce.

Thinking back to the pages of Al's journal, I thought maybe Adele was responsible for his French maid fetish.

Kate continued with her story. "But Bert was persistent, and finally Adele agreed to go out with him. During dinner, he told her he would like to start seeing her but she had to choose between him and his ex-wife. He feels very self-important, as you know. Adele was not willing to risk her friendship with Joyce. Bert was crestfallen. Never had he envisioned her turning him down. Striking out with her was a big blow to his ego. Someone heard him say once that he thought women would gravitate to him like flies to sugar now that he was divorced. Apparently Al tried to call Adele many times after her refusal, but she would not take his calls. But he's never really given up. She still sees his number on caller ID every now and then."

I was shocked, both by his behavior and by the fact that so many people knew about it. There I was, being discreet about our breakup out of respect for his good standing in the community, and it turned out that nearly everyone knew he was a skirt chaser. He would have been very surprised at the gossip he was generating and how fast it had spread through the village.

Soon it became time for me to hit the road if I wanted to make the art show by mid-afternoon. "Please plan a trip to New Haven for a visit," I said to my friends as we hugged each other good-bye. "Or we could plan a shopping spree in New York. We haven't been to Bloomingdale's in ages. A trip to Boston to hear the Pops would be fun, too, especially during the Christmas holidays."

We agreed to check our schedules and make a date soon. I left feeling extremely lucky to have such great friends in my corner.

My friends had further piqued my interest in Al's shenanigans, so after returning home and eating a light dinner, I once again sat down with the journal. I had no intention of sharing its contents with anyone, but I was curious to learn more about the man who had become a complete mystery to me. Unfortunately, there was nothing enlightening in its pages. If I thought it would offer me some kind of understanding or reveal a newfound self-awareness on Al's part, I was wrong. Reading about his sexual adventures in his journal was more than enough. The man badly needed something to interest him other than who would be his next conquest. The man had a one-track mind. Like a young man in the throes of puberty, he seemed to have no interests outside of sexual conquest.

I picked up where I'd left off, with Al's description of a blind date after he answered a promising-looking ad in the newspaper's personal column. After the woman in the ad agreed to have dinner with him, they set the time and place. He couldn't have been more disappointed. The woman was plump, dressed in a dowdy manner, and during dinner he noticed "with horror" the hairs on her double chin. To add insult to injury, she was also taller than he was. There wasn't one thing about the woman that was exciting, he wrote, not even her contributions to their conversation. He was sorely disappointed in the outcome, and decided that answering personal ads was not the way to meet women. That first date would be his last date. He ended the entry by scribbling, *That's what I get for buying a pig in a poke.*

His next dating adventure started off more promising. This woman was very attractive and younger than Al. He had heard she was a fairly new widow, and he thought by now she was probably lonely and in need of a man. The restaurant was upscale, with white tablecloths and napkins, sparkling glassware, and flowers on every table. The very moment they sat down she began to talk. And talk. All about her deceased husband, how wonderful he was, and how much she missed him. No way Al could compete with a sainted ghost. So as soon as he took her home, he took off like a rocket. *I tried to be so charming to her but nothing I did worked*, he wrote.

I was fully aware of how charming he could be. At one time, he could charm me right out of my panties. The man seemed to never give up, but I'm sure that consoling a still grieving widow was not in his plans.

I closed the book after reading that. I had read enough for one day. Al's obsession with seduction was exhausting.

As I escaped by painting, I thought about Al and his shenanigans. Getting my mind off our past was hard to do. I think I was still trying to understand him and why he acted the way he did. He seemed to select lonely women whom he thinks have been waiting for someone just like him to come along. Was that why he had asked me to live with him? The women would be disappointed in that he wanted more than companionship. Not many women would like his lifestyle. However, he thinks he is irresistible and cannot fathom why women tell him no.

I got another call from Al just before Thanksgiving. I don't know why I picked up the phone. Maybe I was feeling generous because the holidays were approaching. The conversation started off pleasant enough. He actually asked how I was doing, shared some info about a book he thought I might find interesting, and told me about a sculpture he was working on and planned to exhibit.

Soon enough, however, he started whining to me about some women he'd met recently. He could not understand why they were rejecting his overtures. He thought himself a great catch. After all, he said to me, Carol had called him her stud muffin. (Al did not know that I was reading his journal. I would never tell him, either. If he missed the diary he never mentioned it, nor did he ask me about it.)

I told Al I really didn't want to hear about these women.

"But I'm not telling you to make you upset. I truly want your advice. You know me better than just about any woman I've been with." Then he brought up Adele, how it frustrated him that he couldn't win her over.

"Al, I really don't know what to say—"

"Okay, so here's the thing, Maddie. I have been so disappointed and distraught that I've sought help from a new psychologist."

"You mean for your obsessive need to seduce every woman you meet?" I asked.

"No, I need to know what I'm doing wrong—why I can't seem to win these women over."

I couldn't help but laugh. "Well, let's hope this one tells you the problem is that you're stuck in an adolescent mind-set. Al, your sexual pursuits aren't *normal*."

But I couldn't make him listen. Apparently, his current psychologist had told him to do whatever pleased him and not to feel guilty about it. He was entitled to pursue his happiness. If one woman rejected him, move on to the next.

Great. Now a *professional* was justifying Al's actions. I told Al I was uninterested in the direction the conversation was taking, wished him luck, and hung up the phone. He would never learn.

Chapter Twenty-One

THANKSGIVING AND CHRISTMAS CAME and went quietly. After New Year's I began to put away the Christmas decorations and get the house back in order. It was then that I discovered a pack of vacation photos that I had never put in an album. Browsing through them brought back happy memories. Al and I were smiling or laughing in almost every photo, our arms around each other or holding hands. *Were we ever really that happy?* I wondered. Yes, I do believe we were. However, our lives had played out and the curtain closed on the stage of his estate.

I needed to get back to Oak Ridge to pick up some paintings I'd neglected to take with me and that I needed for an upcoming show. Al was storing them in the basement, but I hadn't had the heart until now to actually go back to the house. I felt stronger now, though, and thought that Al would even like some of these photos. I gave him a call, told him about them, and reminded him that I still had some paintings to pick up. "I thought I could kill two birds with one stone. Bring you some photos, take my paintings."

Al told me that was fine. I could come up on Saturday if I wanted. He didn't have any plans.

The weather was freezing, but while I dreaded leaving my cozy house, neither did I look forward to being cooped up. I had already shoveled and de-iced the driveway, and the roads had been plowed clear. No reason not to set out for Oak Ridge.

Upon arrival I rang the door and waited for Al to open it. I wasn't sure how to greet him. Was I supposed to extend a businesslike handshake? Give him a hug? A kiss on the cheek? I'd been much more relaxed with him in New York City, but I was embarrassed to be in his presence since reading his journal and learning about his goings-on from my friends. Al solved the problem for me by answering the door and holding it wide open, ushering me in with an exaggerated swoop of his right arm.

"I apologize for intruding on your weekend," I said. "I hope I didn't interrupt any plans. But I have a show soon and really need to frame these paintings. If you don't mind, I'll just run down into the basement and get them."

I was having a difficult time looking him in the eye. He was my former lover and the love of my life, but I felt more than ever that I was in the presence of a stranger.

"Of course I don't mind," he replied, walking me into the living room. "I'll give you a hand. But have a seat first. I want to look at the photos. Can I get you anything to drink?"

I shook my head no and took a seat on the sofa in front of the fire. The sofa replaced the one I took with me, and I was surprised at how nice it was. Did Al suddenly develop some taste in furniture, or did one of his women help him pick it out? I pushed the thought from my mind.

Al sat next to me and held out a hand for the photos. "I've been look- ing forward to seeing these. It was such a fun trip." Then he cocked his head. "Gee, Maddie, I haven't seen you in ages. You look great. Is that a new outfit? And your jewelry is really flattering, too."

I can't remember Al ever commenting on the way I looked except to complain about it. He must have been as nervous as I was.

I sat quietly while he turned his attention to the stack of photos, making a comment here and there. Then he set them aside and asked if

I could give him some input on the gallery. He had decided to complete my project.

I smiled and nodded, trying to be as amicable as he was. But I knew I was only playacting. Sitting there talking to him, looking around at all that I had accomplished in his house, I could feel my anger at how he'd treated me bubbling just beneath my calm exterior. I gritted my teeth as he walked me through the portion of the house that I'd cordoned off as the future gallery. He was making progress. I could see that it would be a beautiful, light-filled space. Once it would have held my work as well as his. That rankled. I needed to get my paintings and get out of there before I either started to cry or yell. I excused myself and went to get my things before I said hateful things. After all, I was a guest in his house now, and I no longer had a right to fuss with him.

Muffin came into the room, wagging his tail amiably. He ambled over to me and put his head on my lap. When I began scratching him he rolled on his back and sighed. The sweet dog was showing his age. His movements were not as spry as usual. I had pampered him when I lived there, and we missed each other. George was nowhere to be seen, but then again he had always been mostly an outdoor cat.

Just then Al's cell phone rang. I jumped. Boy, was that a familiar sound, and an unpleasant one at that. He held up a finger to tell me to hang on a minute, but I just shook my head, gave Muffin a final scratch, and headed down to the basement.

When I returned to the living room, a painting in each hand, Al was still on the phone. He'd completely forgotten about his offer to help me.

"Al, I'm leaving now," I said loudly. Now it was his turn to jump. Again, I got a finger. But I just yelled a quick good-bye as I walked out the door, leaving him chatting with whoever it was who was more important than I. He hadn't changed one bit.

Back in the car, I let out a long, loud scream. I was angry not only with Al but also with myself. The phone call set off memories of other phone calls and the hurt they had caused. He was up to his same old tricks, but I had also put myself in this situation, once again thinking that I could handle it. Seeing him only dredged up deep-seated emotions that were better left buried. At one time I didn't think that I could live without him. Now, knowing that I no longer lived with him, that I was no longer on the sidelines of his life, was the most freeing thing I've ever felt. Once I got home, I sent Al an e-mail thanking him for letting me come by, telling him he could keep the photographs, and asking please never to call me again. After all these years I could finally say that I was very tired of him. Indeed, we had become strangers to each other. Now that we no longer lived together, I felt like a burden had been lifted. I kept asking myself how long I had felt so heavily burdened.

So what did Al do? He sent me an e-mail in response.

"How about we communicate this way?" he wrote. "It will be much better. We won't be able to see or hear tempers flare, but we can still stay in touch and see how each other is doing."

Now another question entered my mind. I had been so busy trying to figure out what kept me tethered to Al that I hadn't bothered to wonder what kept him tethered to *me*. If his newfound swinging single lifestyle was so compelling, why was he trying to keep up a relationship with me? Did he truly care about my well-being, or was this just another case of him being unable to accept rejection, even from a woman he didn't love and didn't want to be with?

I needed to put a stop to this. Changing my e-mail and phone number would be a major hassle, but I'd do it if I didn't have any other choice.

"Al, too much has happened between us," I e-mailed back. "We can't be friends. And to be honest, I'm tired of talking with you. For some reason you insist on rubbing your sexual escapades in my face, and I find it disgusting. You are abnormal. Find another confidant. You really don't care how I'm feeling or how my life is going. Please stop corresponding with me."

But he didn't stop. The e-mails kept coming. In one, he told me how lonely and bored he was. In another he had the audacity to suggest I accompany him to New York City for a couple days. In yet another he went on and on about his conflicting feelings for Carol. While he definitely thought she was crazy, he didn't want to give her up. She was too good in bed. I wondered if, based on Al's journal entry, Carol had resumed her campaign to move in with Al. I doubt she had any idea of the women who regularly revolved in and out of Al's front door. Al did not get a response to any of these e-mails from yours truly. The delete key had become my new best friend.

After my visit to Twin Oaks Manor, I went to Danbury to work and to put my boutique up for sale with a local agent. Selling the shop would make my life simpler, but it was a difficult decision to make. My employees put my inventory on sale and prepared for the closing. These people were special, and I had enjoyed our relationship and friendship. They were also good at their jobs and would not have any problem finding new ones. As for nursing, I still wasn't ready to retire yet. I enjoyed the part-time work and my patients, and I needed the extra income. I was not counting pennies for the present, just saving dollars for the future. After my work period was over for the next week, I drove back to New Haven and continued my life there.

Even though I knew nothing good could come from it, I continued to read Al's journal. In many ways, what he wrote would have been funny had it not been so sad. Some of his dalliances had occurred before I lived with him, but much of it had occurred during our five years together. That surprising knowledge really was hurtful. How had I been so blind to what was going on under my own roof? I had never suspected, so I wasn't looking for evidence. I trusted him. Reading about his failed conquests, I could only assume they were part of the reason why he invited me to live with him. Perhaps Carol and I were the only women dumb enough to take him up on his invitation. The other women were smarter than we were when it came to men. I don't like admitting this, even to myself.

One entry described a visit from Ginger during a weekend I was away working—the same woman with whom he'd planned a rendezvous immediately after we returned from South Carolina. Turns out that Ginger had canceled their weekend because she felt guilty about her significant other. Al had told me that. And that Ginger was out of his life for good because of it. How did he remember who was revolving in and out his door and who was due when? It boggles one's mind. Did he think women stood in line singing "Kum-Ba-Ya" when they saw him? Holding on to all his women's affections was important to him. But there she was, in my home, only a few months later. Al described her as being the opposite of Carol: younger, taller, with curly red hair, alabaster skin marred only by a smattering of freckles. Most importantly, he wrote, she had a bombshell figure, the opposite of Carol's more athletic build.

I know she's a natural redhead, too, he wrote. *It's the same color everywhere.*

How crass and crude is that? Obviously, he was either suffering from some kind of double personality or he did a great job of hiding his true self from others. Why in the world did he feel the need to write about a body area? He had become a dirty old man and not the polite gentleman whom I had known him to be. He had never said in my presence the kinds of things he'd written in his journal. He cursed on occasion, but he was never trashy. His deceit was distressing. Had he always been that way, or did he change only recently? The thought that I'd spent much of my life in love with Dr. Jekyll when he was really Mr. Hyde made me almost sick to my stomach. But Al and his psychologist think he was just being a "normal" male.

And for all his drive to seduce these women, he wasn't very nice to them on the page. Al went on to write that Ginger, while mentally stable, suffered from "extreme" emotional instability (talk about the pot calling the kettle black) and drama in her personal life that caused her to cry at the drop of a hat.

I'm sure Ginger had to feel some guilt about cheating on her significant other with Al, or at the very least was torn between the two.

Al hates competition. He couldn't fully commit to these women, yet he demanded 100 percent loyalty from them. He is not good at providing emotional support. No wonder Ginger was "unstable."

In one entry Al wrote quite a bit about Ginger, maybe even more than he did about Carol. I read with interest another entry. Al had indulged in one of his favorite winter activities: a steaming hot sauna followed by, assuming it had recently stormed, a dive into the freshly fallen snow to make snow angels. I suppose I don't need to point out that he does this in the nude. That day he failed to notice a fairly large tree branch buried only a few inches beneath the snow. While moving his arms, he scraped his shoulder and pulled the muscle.

The pain was intense, but Al was determined not to let it get in the way of his fun. When Ginger arrived he suggested a sauna as the perfect way for her to relax after her long drive. Plus, the hot steam would be good for his pulled muscle, although he did not let on that he was hurt. He didn't want anything to interfere with their sex. After the long sauna, they returned to the house, wrapped in towels and hungry for dinner. Apparently Ginger was an excellent cook.

At this point Al's writing took an unusually circumspect turn. All he says is that they enjoyed a great dinner, lively conversation, and then went to bed. Nothing about what they actually did there.

He didn't write much about what they did the next day either, except to say that he and Ginger went for a snow-trek in the late afternoon before returning home to dress for dinner. Al, who didn't get out much, was excited about the prospect of showing off this young, beautiful woman to his neighbors.

He described the meal: *The restaurant served traditional German fare. I ordered split pea soup, bratwurst, sauerkraut, and potatoes—my favorite. The servings were generous and deliciously prepared. But the meal had embarrassing repercussions for me.*

I laughed out loud. Why on earth did he order that meal? He knows pea soup causes his stomach to ache in the best of circumstances, violent diarrhea in the worst. I didn't need to guess which it was this time. His frequent trips to the restroom must have been embarrassing.

But that was Al for you, not wanting to admit his physical shortcomings to anyone. He must keep up his youthful persona regardless of the cost.

Alas, the weekend went by all too quickly, Al wrote. He was excited about the prospect of seeing her again soon, though. *Ginger can really get my juices flowing. She's good for me. She makes me feel young.*

Again, if it hadn't been so sad, it would have been funny. It read like a soap opera, only one for middle-aged men seeking to recapture their lost youth.

Chapter Twenty-Two

MARGARET CAME UP for a visit in mid-February and broke some news to me about Al. Apparently, he and Ginger, who had become quite the item, were now on the outs. One of Margaret's coworkers knew Ginger well and shared the story.

A couple weekends before, Ginger drove up, and she and Al took a proper tour around the village. I can imagine how picturesque it must have been, given there had just been a heavy snowfall. It was a quaint, friendly, and very pretty village. The population is less than two thousand. That day, with the fresh snow, I know the picturesque streets and woods resembled a Currier and Ives Christmas card. As they were walking around, Al pointed out different points of interest and gave her a brief history. All seemed to be going well until Ginger suddenly began to cry. She wanted to talk seriously about her future with Al.

Al supposedly shut her down, saying that as far as he was concerned their relationship had not progressed enough to warrant a talk about the future. Besides, what was wrong with the way it was?

I could just see it. Poor Ginger snorting and sniffling, Al cringing because he hates emotional outbursts, trying to tell her he liked everything just fine as it was.

That set Ginger off. She told Al that unless he was willing to commit to her they were finished. She would no longer be just a sexual plaything. She confided to Margaret's coworker that while sex with Al had been passionate in the past, lately things had begun to sag a bit in the bedroom. She could overlook that because she loved him. But she saw now that he didn't care for her and probably never would. It was time to end their affair.

Al took her back to Twin Oaks, where she packed her things and left, telling him she was embarrassed she ever let their affair get this far. Then she asked him never to contact her again. Al must have been stunned.

I didn't know what to say to Margaret about Ginger except good riddance. I knew from his journal that Al really enjoyed this woman. He thought she was good for him, but obviously he was not good for her. What else was new? It was all about him, same as always. I was glad that Ginger at least had the strength to get out of his life. She was wise to walk away when she did.

A few days after my lunch with Margaret, Al broke my rule about no phone calls and left a frantic message on my cell phone to call him immediately. It was urgent. Against my better judgment, and thinking that maybe something terrible had happened, I returned his call.

As usual, he launched right in without even a hello. "I'm going to take the girls skiing in a couple weeks, but the sitter isn't able to stay with Muffin and George. Would you stay here and look after them? Muffin has not been well, and I hate to put him in a boarding kennel."

Way to pull on my heartstrings, Al, I thought. He knew that I loved the old dog and that he loved me. During the five years I spent living with Al, I had come to regard Muffin and George as my own. It was with a heavy heart that I had to turn Al down. "Sorry, your animals are not my responsibility. Have you tried to find someone local to look after him?"

"No, I thought you would come here," he said. I could just picture him pouting at the other end of the line. "I know you love them, so I thought you would be glad to do it."

He then went on and on about how he and the girls really needed some father-daughter time. The slopes were in great condition, so the timing was perfect. He also said that since he would be skiing, he had not planned to teach on Thursday. I wondered why he felt the need to tell me all this in such detail. His trip had nothing to do with me.

"Sorry, Al. I'm sure you can find someone else. There's always the kennel, much as you hate to do that."

Before hanging up, I reminded him of our agreement. "Please, stop calling me."

One Saturday about a month later, feeling much better after being cooped up with a head cold for most of the week, I decided to take a walk to the post office. I had started to make jewelry in my spare time and was sending one of my first pieces to my sister for her birthday. I wanted to get the package in the mail as soon as possible. The house was tidy, and the weather was perfect for an outing. The bright mid-afternoon sun felt wonderful, almost like a natural sauna. Once at the post office, I bumped into Elaine, the wife of one of Al's colleagues. We began to chat, and then she suggested tea at a café around the corner.

Elaine and I had always been friendly, but I hadn't spoken to her in nearly a year. I felt she was a friend anyway. During our tea she told me that she heard that I was living in New Haven and that Bert and I were no longer together. I confirmed her knowledge. She offered her condolences on my split with Al and then asked if I was seeing anyone.

"No, I'm happy being single for now," I replied.

I asked about her husband, and she replied, "Dan's doing fine. His workload has eased up now that he's no longer covering for Al during his trip away."

"I heard about that. I'm glad Al and his daughters had some time together."

Elaine furrowed her brows at me. "They went to the Bahamas, too?"

There was that sinking feeling in my stomach again. "What do you mean?"

Elaine blushed and looked down at her hands. "I guess there's nothing wrong with me telling you, but a woman named Sondra invited Bert on a trip to the Bahamas to escape the cold for a few days. I think they met somewhere in the Berkshires at an art opening, and they struck up a friendship that turned romantic. Sondra's apparently got a bit of money. She paid all their traveling expenses, including first-class tickets."

I didn't say anything, so Elaine continued with her story. "Their trip home was a disaster. You remember that Arctic blast that blew through here and closed all the airports? Well, Al and Sondra's flight home from Miami was canceled because of it. Al called Dan to tell him that he was stranded in Miami and to please cover his class for a couple more days. He had told Dan he was going skiing, too. Gave him a big sob story about how desperately he wanted to spend time with his daughters. It wasn't until he was back home that he gave Dan the full details."

I surprised Elaine by bursting out laughing. Boy, was I glad I hadn't agreed to watch the animals. I assured her that I wouldn't tell Al that I knew about his Bahamas trip. I'm sure he believed his secret was safe from everyone but Dan.

"What in the world is he trying to prove, and who is he trying to prove it to?" Elaine asked.

"To tell you the truth, I have no idea," I responded. "I no longer understand him."

After spending another twenty minutes or so catching up, Elaine and I said our good-byes. It was less sunny and warm than when I'd left the house, so I walked home quickly. But it had been a good afternoon. My package to my sister was in the mail, and I had yet more evidence that my decision to leave Al had been the right one.

April was much warmer, so I went down to Oak Ridge Village for a visit. I happened to run into Alice, another friend of mine from the village, and we decided to have lunch to catch up. Alice is a professor of English at a local college, and she, too, apparently knew about Al's trip to the

Bahamas. Obviously, Dan wasn't the only person Al had bragged to, but Sondra, who lives near Oak Ridge, hadn't kept her mouth shut either.

"Bert was enchanted with Sondra, who is young and very pretty," Alice said. "He bragged that she had a lot of money and had treated him to a really good time—so he was sure that she really cared for him."

I rolled my eyes.

"But wait until you hear the good part," Alice said. "Turns out that Sondra bragged to her friends that *Al* is the one who has a ton of money. After all, someone with a house that big, with so much land, and a professorship at Yale had to be loaded, right? So she funded the entire trip, went into debt and everything, to make Al fall for her. Sure enough, Al was so smitten he came *this close* to asking her to move in with him. But when he discovered that she only wanted him for what she thought was his money, he sent her on her way. Can you believe it?"

"My word, they really almost deserved each other, didn't they?" I asked.

Alice laughed. "And he's *always* on the make. He even hit on me a couple months ago."

When she saw the look on my face, she stretched an arm across the table and patted me on the hand. "Don't worry, this ends well."

She began by saying, "I mistakenly thought Bert was harmless. He asked me to come by his house to edit a paper he had written and then invited me to stay for dinner. I didn't mind editing his paper, and sharing a meal with someone would be nice, since I usually ate by myself."

While she was editing, she said, Al kept coming over to where she sat and would put his arm around her shoulder. The first time he did it, she found it friendly, an almost fatherly gesture. But the second or third time, he let his hand linger at the top of her back, making a small caressing motion. That made her uncomfortable.

"I said to him, 'Al, I'm trying to work. Do you mind leaving me alone until I'm finished?'"

Once finished, he invited her into the kitchen for a glass of wine before dinner. The edit had taken nearly ninety minutes—it was a long paper—and her neck was cramped. She accepted the drink, knowing that a little bit of alcohol would help untense her muscles. When Al saw her rub her neck, he came over and tried to massage it. "I told him I was fine, but it really struck me as odd."

She finished her wine quickly, hoping that dinner would come sooner rather than later.

"I told him it smelled really good in there, and I asked how much longer for dinner. He told me an hour or so, then offered me another glass."

An alarm went off inside her head. "I said to myself, *Alice, I think Bert is trying to get you drunk.* And there's only one reason to try and do that to a woman."

She could have left right then and there, made some excuse, but she decided to turn the tables on him. Knowing that Al himself had never been a heavy drinker, she kept plying *him* with wine, while she only pretended to drink. She knew it wouldn't take much to put him to sleep.

As Al was cooking, he began to get more and more tipsy, more and more flirty, making suggestive comments. At one point he asked her seductively how he looked in his apron. "He even asked me if I thought he should take off his clothes and wear only the apron, because things were 'heating up' in there. It took everything I had not to laugh."

Instead, Alice played along, made a couple of suggestive comments to string him along, easily avoiding his hands and arms when he tried to touch her.

At one point she thought she would have to give up and leave because everything was taking too long and she was getting more and more disgusted by the minute. She was playing a role that she had never had to play with a man, and never wanted to again. Acting was not on her list of attributes. But she really wanted to teach the old goat a lesson.

"Finally, with the roast in the oven, Al looked at me and said he needed to sit down for just a minute. He went into the living room, and wouldn't you know it? Within minutes he was passed out on the sofa."

Alice went into the kitchen to turn off the stove, regretting the waste of what would likely have been a delicious and pleasant dinner, had Al only behaved himself. Then she went into the guest bathroom to use the facility before heading out the door. A bottle of bright red polish on the counter gave her another idea.

"I went into the living room and polished his finger- and toenails!" Alice said. We both burst out laughing. "I declare, I could have done anything to him. He was out like a light. For a second, because he'd kept calling me 'honey' and 'sugar' all night, I thought of giving him some sugar for real. I saw honey on the counter and poured it in his hair and beard. Too bad the honey wasn't Gorilla Glue! I placed a flower from the bouquet across his abdomen. Wouldn't it have been funny if I had poured honey down his pants? But I didn't want to see *that.*"

I knew for sure she didn't, but I didn't tell her why. Back before Al and I left for South Carolina, I noticed a box of black hair dye in the trash. It wasn't mine, and I had no idea what Al could want with it. Then one night I found out. Turns out he was dying his pubic and scrotal hair black. I didn't have the heart to tell him his private parts looked like a turkey buzzard, with the white penis in the center of all that black.

"The last thing I did before leaving the house was to write a note thanking him for an 'interesting' evening," Alice said. "I would have been happy to never see the smarmy old bastard again, and I have avoided him whenever I could. He never mentioned the evening to me, never called again. I like to think that he hung his head in shame once he woke up, but I doubt he was embarrassed at all."

We had a good laugh over it all, and I marveled at her bravery. I doubt I would have even thought of it.

She was braver than I would have been. I shared with her the tale of Al and the vacation mosquitoes.

As Alice and I finished our food, we both laughed out loud at the antics. People stared at us, but we didn't care.

Maybe someday Al would learn that not every woman thought he was a gift. I had no idea his philandering was this bad, although I believe he had more failures than success. Knowing him, the failures were merely temporary setbacks.

Chapter Twenty-Three

THAT AFTERNOON AFTER I'D RETURNED to New Haven, I found an e-mail from Al waiting in my inbox. I glanced at it briefly, something about Crazy Carol, as Al was still calling her, coming for another visit. Why was this man still bothering me with this nonsense?

I fired off an immediate response, asking him what motive he had for sharing this kind of information with me. Was he asking my permission? Trying to make me jealous? Really, it was all so tiring.

I didn't get a response back until late Monday. In his e-mail, Al outlined a bizarre story. When he picked Carol up from the train station, he noticed that she had a strange look in her eyes and was not acting as animated as she usually did. Since it was near lunchtime, they stopped for a sandwich at a neighborhood café before heading to the house. During their meal, Carol told Al that she loved him and thought they should move in together. Al was speechless. Carol pressed the point. When he finally found his tongue, he told her no. Neither said anything further.

Carol remained silent during the drive to the house. Al could not explain what it was that was different about her—he just knew something was off. Once inside, he started to hug and kiss her. When he tried to feel her breasts and remove her clothes, she went berserk, flailing her arms at him and screaming, "No!"

Perplexed, Al stepped back immediately.

"You have no interest in me as a person," she screamed. She was sobbing now as well. "You are just using me for sex. You are just like Randy." Randy was her ex-husband.

Al saw that as a red flag. Any mention of Randy usually sent her mood plummeting, but this was something else entirely. Then Carol began to peer out the windows and check to see if all the doors were locked. She seemed genuinely afraid that someone was outside and trying to break into the house and hurt her. Al had left the television on before leaving that afternoon, and now a loud male voice boomed from the speakers. Carol thought it was her husband. She stared intensely at the screen and started whispering gibberish. Suddenly, she picked up her cell phone and yelled into it, "Leave me alone! Stop calling me!" The phone had not rung.

Al tried to calm her down, but if he got even a few feet from her, she lashed out and screamed at him to stay away. This went on for at least an hour, with Al speaking to her calmly and trying to get her to sit down and accept a glass of water. She accused him of trying to poison her.

For the first time in their relationship, Al was genuinely scared. He nearly called the hospital, thinking she'd had a psychotic break, but he couldn't imagine what the neighbors would think, an ambulance screaming down the road and EMTs leading a hysterical Carol from the house. Finally, she appeared to be wearing out and coming around. She even allowed Al to lead her upstairs, where he put her to bed and stayed with her until morning.

The next morning, subdued and embarrassed, she tried to apologize. She told Al she just loved him so much, she couldn't imagine life without him.

I tell you what, Maddie, that wasn't heartsick. That was mind sick. Al wrote toward the end of his e-mail. *I couldn't get her to the train station fast enough. I did wait for the train to leave because I didn't know if she would get off or not. Her instability scared the crap out of me. You warned me, but I had no idea. That was Carol's last visit. Our affair is over. I don't want to have anything to do with a crazy woman, sexy or not.*

I thought long and hard before I replied. Then I decided to call him. He needed to hear the tone of my voice.

"Al, I am sorry about Carol," I said when he picked up. "I hate to say I told you so, but I did try to explain how serious her illness is. You just do not listen. You go merrily on your way, doing whatever you want, never thinking about the repercussions. You have been in denial about Carol for a long time. Now maybe you will face her reality. You should have faced it years ago. You have been so smitten with her that you could not or did not want to see the danger signs."

There was silence at the other end of the line. Finally, I'd left Al speechless.

"And for the last time, please stop contacting me about your dalliances. If you need to talk, see your psychologist. If you persist, I will be forced to change my number and my e-mail."

I heard Al sigh. "Maddie, I thought you might be concerned about me, but I can see that you just don't care."

The man was maddening! "No, Al, I don't," I said, nearly screaming at him. "And if you do lose your mind and have Carol over for another visit, please watch the water in the bathroom. You don't need another flood."

Then I hung up the phone. Let him chew on *that*.

One day when I was having lunch at a café near the shopping mall, a colleague of Al's entered, waved, ordered his lunch, and came over and asked if he could share my table. Matthew was a professor of graphic design at the Yale School of Art. His office and Al's were located near each other, so they'd become friendly over the years. He asked how Al was doing. I didn't go into specifics, but I did tell him that we were no longer together and I was now living in New Haven while I made plans to relocate.

"I'm sorry to hear about your breakup, Maddie," he said. "I haven't seen you around campus very much and didn't even realize that until I saw you today. You used to always bring goodies to Al's office, and he was kind enough to share them with me. My wife would do that, too, but with the three children running around her feet, she doesn't get much chance anymore."

"How are Frances and the children?" I asked.

"Everyone is well, thanks. We escaped most of the winter's ailments. A sniffle here and a cough there is about all. Being cooped up with three children is hard on Frances, though. I try to help her out all I can. I would go insane if I had to do it all the time. She's really remarkable."

We continued to chat pleasantly, and then the bell over the door rang. Low and behold, there was Al. I had no idea that he ever ate there. Maybe he was on the prowl again. I turned my head away, but not quickly enough. He saw me.

After placing his order at the counter, he came over to our table. The jerk had the nerve to bend down like he was going to kiss me, but I drew back and moved my head. Then he put a hand on my shoulder, and I slowly shrugged him off. I was aware that Matthew was watching us intently. No telling what he thought, but I was obviously uncomfortable. There was a time when I craved Al's touch. Now, the thought of it repulsed me.

"It's good to see you, Maddie," Al said, smiling at me. "You look very pretty today. When are you coming back to Twin Oaks? I miss you, and you're welcome any time."

I just stared at him.

Then he turned his attention to Matthew. "How are things with you? Everything in the department going well? Did you know I am thinking of retiring soon? Maddie and I will have more time for each other."

I couldn't believe my ears. The nerve of him, acting so possessive. I think I would have preferred that he curse me out. Matthew was the only thing preventing me from slinging a few choice words of my own at Al. I didn't want to embarrass the poor man or make him regret his kindness by creating a scene.

So I said, as sweet as could be, "Al, what are you doing here? Meeting a date? I'm sure your social life is as active as usual, so I can't imagine you've missed me. At the moment I have no plans to go to the Berkshires. I still have friends there, and we get together every so often. The gossip has been interesting. Alice, especially, seems to know *everything*."

Al cleared his throat and was about to say something when I noticed his pager was flashing. "Oh, look. Your lunch is ready. You should pick it up before it gets cold."

Al smiled weakly and said his good-byes.

I could tell Matthew wanted to say something, but I spoke before he could open his mouth. Discussing what had just transpired was not on my agenda for the day. Al's penchant for womanizing was well known, and it had already tarnished what was otherwise a stellar reputation. No need to add more fuel to the fire. "Well, Matthew, it was good to see you again," I said, packing up and leaving a tip on the table. "I enjoyed our visit. Please give Frances my regards, and hug the children for me."

I made sure to avoid looking at Al as I left. Who knew what he would have inferred from the eye contact? I knew there were many men out there who were womanizers, who cheated on their wives and their girl-friends, who thought they were gifts to the opposite sex. But that didn't make it right, nor did it excuse Al's behavior. And therapy didn't seem to be doing him a bit of good. I was just thankful I was no longer tangled in his web, no longer powerless against his manipulative behavior. Six or seven months ago, at my weakest, I likely would have taken Al's comments as evidence of hope. Now I knew better. They were nothing more than evidence of just how delusional he'd become.

Chapter Twenty-Four

IN EARLY MAY I received an invitation from Al to attend a reception at the New-York Historical Society celebrating those homes recently listed on National Historic Register. Twin Oaks Manor was one of those homes, and Al thought I would like to attend as well, since I had done so much work on the restoration.

I had not spoken to him since our exchange at the café two weeks before. I had grown content with the life I was making for myself and hardly gave him a thought these days. But this *was* a big deal. Six years ago, the house was a shambles. Now, due in large part to my efforts, it had received prestigious recognition as a showpiece. Even Al's huge ego didn't prevent him from saying so. Furthermore, Al wrote, he was getting ready to open the in-house gallery, Falcon Gallery, and he wanted to tell me about the plans.

After thinking about it for a couple days, I wrote back and told Al I would attend the Historical Society gathering. I was proud of the work I'd done and was happy to accept the award. This would also be my first time attending a Historical Society event, and I was curious as to what it entailed.

I arrived late Friday afternoon. The plan was to meet Al at City Center in Manhattan, where the event would be held. I knew then that I had let go of a lot of my emotional attachments and was in a much healthier place.

Al greeted me warmly at the reception. Being in his presence for a social event was strange, and I felt awkward. I never discussed my feeling with Al. I don't know if he was uncomfortable or not. However, we carried on as if all was well between us. We mingled with the other attendees, even though neither of us knew any of them, and actually enjoyed ourselves—until he brought up Carol and Ginger, that is. It seemed to me that talking about his women was the only conversation he knew. His known intellect was missing. I quickly changed the subject.

"Maddie, I want you to know that I don't plan to see either one again. I plan to move on. There are plenty of women out there. I know I can find the right one for me. She is out there just waiting for me."

I was glad for their sakes that they had wised up.

Al, however, was still as dense as ever. "Ginger accused me of being old and impotent. Can you believe that? I think I look better than other men my age. In fact, I don't think I look old at all. I have a lot of good years left. I just need the right woman."

I rolled my eyes but kept my mouth shut. No sense in telling him that he looked like a rapidly aging man to me. His lifestyle was taking its toll, but he hung tight to the image of himself as a youthful and sexy stud with whom every woman was just dying to jump into bed. I shut him out. Al seemed to have a need to vent, but why me, for goodness sakes? I suppose at that point I should have been viewing him as a patient rather than an ex-lover. He would have made a great case study.

Listening to him go on and on about his attempts to preserve his youth was exhausting as well. The diets, the workouts, the Botox injections, the hair dyeing, the laser treatments to remove the liver spots on his hands, the beard to hide his sagging neck, and all for what? He was *still* aging. He had never been the swinger he had thought himself to be. When he was younger, I thought he was sexy, but that wasn't what I loved about him.

Finally, Al stopped prattling on about his various regimens and mentioned the Falcon Gallery. That got my attention. He was ready for the opening the next day, he said.

"I have tried to set up everything like I think you would have, using your plans and ideas. The gardens and grounds are not up to your standards, but I think they're fine for now. The house is beautiful, though; it looks the best it has in years."

No mention of inviting me. Nor did I hear the words, "Thank you. I appreciate all you've done." Apparently, they didn't exist in his vocabulary.

Then Al told me he had a date the next day for lunch. Apparently he was taking Adele to lunch at the Brewery. That five-star restaurant happened to be my favorite, and Al was well aware of that. We had gone there on many special occasions.

Al looked at me and saw how shocked I was. "Oh, don't worry. I plan to be back in plenty of time to prepare for the opening reception."

"What an egotistical jerk you are, Al. Why would I worry about that?" I asked, furious. And I wasn't jealous of Adele, although I did wonder what had happened to her resolve to stay away from Al for good. But, no, she could have him and all his problems. What made me angry was that he had used my plans for the gallery, including the logo I'd designed many years ago, without asking or even thanking me. And to add insult to injury, he was celebrating that opening by taking another woman to a restaurant that for many years we'd considered our special place.

All too late, I realized he had only wanted me to come to the Historical Society reception so that he could pick my brain about other ideas I might have had for the gallery opening. What a user he was! Once again, I was devastated. I had fallen for yet another one of his ploys. I would not fall for another one. Never again would I be cajoled into visiting. It seemed that every time I tried to be friendly and helpful, everything backfired. Feeling dejected, I left without saying good-bye. I drove to the main highway toward New Haven without a backward glance. He and Adele could stick that gallery where the sun didn't shine.

Al never did understand what a devastating blow he had dealt me. Before meeting him, I never would have considered living with a man outside of marriage. It's just not how I was raised. It might sound old-fashioned, but I grew up thinking that a man and woman met, fell in love, the man proposed, they got married, had children, and that was that. Funny, given my upbringing, how totally *untraditional* I turned out. I rationalized my deeds by saying that we loved each other and would marry someday. I'm thankful my parents were not alive to see me go through this. I will say, however, that Al was my first and only affair.

In retrospect, I should never have agreed to live with Al without a commitment to marry. And I should not have allowed myself to be caught up in his sweet talk and hollow promises. How naïve I was, to think that a mere *contract* would have given me certain assurances. How businesslike and unromantic. No wonder Al thought nothing of breaking it. No, I should have insisted we marry. Al might have still acted the same way, but at least I would have had certain legal rights. For one thing, Twin Oaks Manor would legally have been half mine. Even though Al owned it before the marriage, we would have spent what was considered joint income on its considerable renovations. Al would have had to buy me out. Sure, money is cold comfort, but at least it's something.

Even though I was blissfully happy in the beginning and it seemed we were destined to become intimate partners for life, I still had nagging doubts every once in a while. I should have listened to them. Instead, I was blinded by love and the age-old belief that if I just loved someone enough they would change.

I realized then that Al had never loved me. I also realized that he likely wasn't capable of loving *anyone*. Although he never hit me, never in any way proved himself to have violent tendencies, he was nonetheless emotionally and mentally abusive. He was a liar, extremely manipulative, and a narcissist to boot. I'm ashamed that I allowed it to go on so long. The only thing that gave me comfort was knowing that I had learned my lesson for good. Al would never learn his.

I heard that the gallery opening was not a success. Only four people showed. I did wonder if my presence would have made a difference. While Al had grown up in the village, I had made many friends while there. They would have attended the opening to show their support for me and the work I had accomplished.

Adele moved in with Al soon after the gallery opening. This was definitely another blow to my ego. He'd had many women, but I was the only one he'd ever asked to live with him.

It took a long time, but I finally woke up and let go of my dreams of a future with Al. The torch that I'd carried for him for thirty years had finally gone out.

If any woman were to ask my advice in affairs of the heart, I would tell them: beware of womanizing men. If you become involved with one, leave. It's a no-win situation. Don't keep holding on because you think they will change or revert back to the loving partners they were at the beginning of your relationship. They are never satisfied. And it's not your fault. Their need for conquest is greater than their love or need for you. What I had experienced with Al sadly occurs in way too many relationships.

Chapter Twenty-Five

By early summer I felt happier than I had in a long time. My plans for moving were falling into place nicely. The housing market was down and prices were lower—it was definitely a good time to buy. But not here. I had decided to retire from nursing and move back South. I gave a two-week notice at work and made an offer on a house in Raleigh, North Carolina, that the sellers had accepted. We would close in four weeks. I had already sold my boutique and hired movers. After I settled in the North Carolina area, I planned on deciding whether I wanted to work as a nurse again. I knew that I would always paint and garden because they're great stress relievers for me. Raleigh offered various cultural opportunities, which I looked forward to discovering.

I sent Al an e-mail telling him I would be moving in five weeks and he could have his house back.

That afternoon the phone rang. It was Al. "Moving? What do you mean moving?" he barked at me. "I thought you would stay there longer and maintain the property. You can't move now, at least not until I find a buyer for that house."

He then had the nerve to ask if I would arrange for any repairs that needed to be done and then find a real estate agent to list the house.

I took a couple deep breaths to remain calm. "No, Al. I will not handle any of that for you. I can't believe you even have the nerve to ask.

I restored one house for you and now another woman gets to enjoy the results of my hard work. As far as I'm concerned, this place can crumble to the ground."

Ignoring me completely, Al said, "Yes, but now is not the time for me to sell the New Haven house. The housing market will make a comeback. I will sell it then. So maybe you can contact a rental agent for me?"

I was dumbfounded. Not only had Al never truly thanked me for the work I did at Twin Oaks or apologized for cheating on me and destroying our relationship, he had grown even more self-centered. As usual, it was all about him. He never even asked where I was moving to.

"I don't plan to do anything for you ever again. Those days are long over, so face reality. You are so uncaring and unthinking where others are concerned. You are one of the most narcissistic people that I have ever known. Your life is all about you and your desires, and my moving and getting on with my life is messing with your plans. Too bad. I'm not going to wait until the time is right for you. I close on my new house in four weeks. In five weeks this house will be vacant for you to do with as you wish."

Then he had the nerve to ask that I stay in touch. "I'd like it if we could still be friends. We can e-mail and talk on the phone from time to time. Maybe you can even come back for a visit."

Why did I even try? "You have no clue, do you, what you've done to me? I can't say it any plainer than this: I have lost all respect for you and I almost lost respect for myself. You want to be friends, but I do not. I gave you all I had to give and it wasn't enough. I don't have anything else to give you. I am through. Our life together is finally finished. Consider this your final good-bye!" I said, and then slammed down the phone.

After all these years, I finally understood that Al's life was all about him and no one else. Never again would I allow him or anyone else to mistreat me. I wanted him to grow up, to accept his inadequacies and go forward pursing happiness as he saw it. But he was almost seventy-one years old. It was likely too late for him to change. Failing that, I wanted him to stay the hell away from me.

I accepted now that very early in our relationship, those twenty-five-plus years ago, there were many women in his life. As much as I hate to admit it, I probably suspected all along. I must have been too wrapped up in our romance or else I would have kicked him across the Berkshires a long time ago. With his inflated ego, he probably would have just bounced from peak to peak.

He always said that none of the women mattered. He was right. His encounters never mattered, nor will they ever. Otherwise he would have been content to settle down and make a successful life with one woman. I wonder now if I'd ever even mattered to him outside of what I could do to make his life more comfortable. I know few women would have done for him what I did. For years, I had seriously tried to understand him. I had helped him through illnesses and with bouts of depression and self-doubt when he struggled with his art. I lived up to our commitment and was a faithful and loving companion. I created a home for us, restoring Twin Oaks and its grounds to its former glory, and I helped get it listed on the National Registry. But while I was building flowerbeds, Al was tearing down the fabric that held our relationship together. Nearly one year after leaving him and about to uproot myself from my life in New England and head back home, Al couldn't even say, "I'm sorry."

By late summer, I was settled into my new home in Raleigh. I moved into a townhouse that required much less maintenance than the New Haven home and the manor. Raleigh is North Carolina's capital city and is therefore larger than Danbury and New Haven. I enjoyed meeting new neighbors and making new friends. I was able to focus on painting and making jewelry since I did not have a lot of house and yard upkeep. I started showing and selling my jewelry and art at local craft shows. My interests kept me busy, so I did not have time to continue my nursing career.

I also found my own therapist, and with her help I began to accept that Al was not only narcissistic but a pathological liar as well. Perhaps even slightly sadistic. But part of overcoming my grief over the death of our affair and Al's ill treatment was to accept the part I played in allowing it to happen. Al is far from perfect, and so am I. As part of my healing, I am learning to forgive myself and to rebuild my self-worth. His emotional abuse and psychological abuse were dangerous, and I am glad I finally removed myself from that unhealthy situation. Admitting that I was emotionally and psychologically abused was not easy. My therapist suggested that perhaps I felt a deep-seated need to suffer and punish myself. I found that hard to believe, since I had come from a loving family, but something drew me to Al and something made me stay. Julie once said that I was Al's doormat. At the time I was insulted and told her so. I don't consider myself weak, irrational, or perverted, but I see now that Al was more than just a simple error in judgment on my part. I hung on to my dream of life with this man for twenty-five years. There has to be a reason for that, so I continued my work with my therapist.

I did begin to like myself again and knew that never again would I set myself up for this kind of hurt. I also on occasion accepted lunch and dinner invitations. I enjoyed the company of these men, but that is as far as I wanted a relationship to go. Every day I was learning something new about myself. That's what I concentrated on: discovering who Madeline was, what she wanted, and where she was going.

I didn't miss the social and economic privileges of being the partner of a high-profile artist and professor. Stability remained high on my list, though, as did reclaiming my emotional strength.

I learned to enjoy being by myself and doing what I wanted to do. Being alone is better than being unhappy. I also learned that I didn't have to be strong all the time, nor did I always have to be a peacemaker. Expressing my emotions is healthy as long as I don't let anger turn to hate. That could destroy me. But I did learn to reclaim my ability to be assertive and to stand up for myself.

As I struggled to understand why I had allowed Al to take such advantage of me, I wondered if perhaps I believed that negative attention was better than no attention at all. After all, unlike many abused women, I was not trapped in the relationship, except emotionally. Money or freedom of movement had never been an issue. But there are all kinds of ways to suffer abuse, and none of them are acceptable.

Epilogue

TWO YEARS HAVE PASSED since I left Al, and my life is completely different now. I am emotionally and mentally stronger than I was when I was with him. I see my life as hopeful and bright rather than as a deep, dark pit of despair out of which I struggle to climb. Knowing that I can deal with problems head-on is a great feeling.

Finding the real Madeline has likewise been wonderful.

My emotional pain is almost completely gone, and I rarely think of my life with Al anymore. Admittedly, when I hear about a scoundrel, he does pop into my head. But the thought of him is not accompanied by grief, just pity. I have come to see him as pathetically sad and a truly unhappy man.

I have heard that since Adele's departure Al has not had a woman live with him. Her leaving was ironic. Al took exotic Adele on a long-awaited trip to Austria but when the time came to return to the United States, she refused to come back with him. She used him to get back to her home country. I wonder how he felt to be rejected again. How he could think that sex was more important than love and friendship is beyond me.

I see a lot of Julie and Joan now, and they tell me I look and act much happier and that my eyes have their old sparkle back. I honestly do not know how I would have survived my breakup with Al without them. Their emotional support was unlimited and invaluable.

Their unflagging support has had another positive outcome as well, influencing me to pursue volunteer work at my local women's shelter. My years of experience as a psychiatric nurse and as an artist have come in handy as a volunteer in a women's shelter, and I've found the work exceptionally rewarding. My heart goes out to those battered souls, many of whom are also with their children, but every day holds its small miracles as well. I work hard to help the women restore their self-esteem, often engaging them in art projects designed to allow them to express themselves in a safe and supportive environment. I work with the younger children on paintings and drawings, while teaching the older children how to make jewelry. Often the children give their creations to their mothers as gifts. It warms my heart to see how pleased the mothers are with their presents, and how much satisfaction the children get from creating and giving them.

If the women are in the shelter long enough, I arrange for local department stores to donate clothing and we put on a fashion show. I think it's important that these women develop a sense of both inner and outer competency. Dressing well not only improves their chances for finding a job, but it is also another important piece in putting back together the puzzle of their self-esteem.

Today, instead of worrying about pleasing Al and anticipating his needs, I worry about pleasing myself and about helping other people. To quote my father, I didn't give "a rat's ass" for Al anymore. Ultimately, the most important thing I learned from Al is how debilitating and isolating narcissism can be. When you spend your entire life focusing on yourself and your petty desires, you not only miss the many wonderful things the world has to offer, you also miss out on making positive and rewarding connections with other people.

I am happy with my new life, and it shows. It is wonderful to wake up every morning with a sense of purpose—to have finally achieved the security, serenity, and well-being that I have longed for my entire life. And I didn't find it in another human being. I found it in myself. I feel like a new person. I *am* a new person.